Olives
Forever

LYNN JOSEPH

BLACK MERMAID PRESS
BOOKS THAT CHALLENGE THE STATUS QUO

Chapter One

BRIDGET

If I hear the name "Jackson" one more time, I'll scream. No boy is worth this kind of headache. Especially when I'm not even dating him!

I finish my text to Ajax with a frustrated emoji and slip my phone back into my pocket.

Ajax won't get my huffy message until he wakes up halfway around the world on his Greek island of olive trees and goats.

I glance around the gymnasium. The Spring Fling Dance is officially happening, and I, Bridget Walker, am a reluctant chaperone.

I can't believe I'm back here at my old stomping grounds. With the dark wood bleachers, too-bright fluorescent lights, and the sound of the *Macarena* being pumped out by the DJ.

The guy hasn't aged a bit. It's the same DJ playing the same songs from five years ago when the *Macerena* was an oldie but goodie and is now a relic that needs to be retired.

Like yours truly.

I still can't believe my sisters talked me into this.

All four of them said I'd make a great chaperone for the high school dance. They're all wrong!

"Oh Bridget, you were popular in school. You went to every dance; you never missed one. This will be a piece of cake. Someone has to make sure neither one of our baby sisters is swept off her feet by that Jackson boy!" That's what my older sister Ava said.

But she's safely in Italy making gelato and falling more in love with her perfect boyfriend, Tyler. Easy for her to toss this mess into my incapable hands.

I don't even know what "swept off your feet" looks like!

And Corrine, the sister after me, the brains of the family, wasn't any better. From her college dorm, she insisted it would be a blast.

Her exact words were, "Bridget, darling, you know you love the spotlight. Being a chaperone at a dance is like being a musical director. You've got this!"

The spotlight? My sisters seem to have forgotten I gave up acting a long time ago.

And what's fun about refereeing a bunch of hormone-overloaded teenagers determined to "get away" with conning the chaperones?

Like the bottle of gin that I found behind the pink punch. Or the gum stuck on the seats of the least popular high school students.

I'm five years out of high school and nothing's changed.

You still have rich kids with their latest fashion, technology, and sneakers. You have the woke crew, picking up soda cans faster than kids can pop one open.

And the wallflowers. The social hopefuls edging the dance floor scoping out gossip to share so they can pull an "in" with the influencers.

And then there are my two youngest sisters, Daisy and Emerald.

Daisy is eighteen, a senior, and in love with Jackson Banza.

Emerald is seventeen, a junior, and in love with . . . you guessed it . . . Jackson Banza.

A boy whose hot-headedness has landed him suspensions, detentions, and a bunch of other *tions* this past year. Including auditions for boyfriend of the year with both my sisters.

See where I'm going with this?

I've been bamboozled into signing up to be a chaperone at this year's Spring Fling for no other reason than to run interference and mother two young women who need a mother.

Ava and Corrine, not to mention Dad, expect me to prevent a supreme meltdown by either Daisy or Emerald when Jackson decides tonight which Alphabet sister he's going to choose.

That's what everyone calls the five Walker sisters, even our father. Because our first names are Ava, Bridget, Corrine, Daisy, and Emerald.

I'm not a gelato master/entrepreneur like Ava.

I'm no freaking book genius like Corrine.

I'm not a writer or a hopeless romantic like Daisy.

I'm not an environmental activist like Emerald.

I'm plain old me, Bridget, a good-time girl, always ready for a night out in Boston with my friends. To see a play, attend a film festival, a concert, or book signing. Anywhere I can absorb art now that I don't create it.

Well, I do create content for a book publisher as my first out of college job. But that's a stop gap. It's not my dream job.

Every other Walker sister has figured out her life passion except for me.

I spend my days scrolling photos, and videos, and reading articles on my phone in the hopes I'll get a brilliant idea of what I'm supposed to be doing with my life.

Right now, my hands itch to take out my phone and see what I've missed in the past fifteen minutes.

I can't be a high school chaperone.

I need a chaperone.

I'd rather drink this half-full bottle of gin I found than report it.

I was voted *Most Likely to Never Settle Down*.

That's how inadequate I am.

I lack the qualities of a mother, a chaperone, and even a girlfriend.

I pull out my phone and text that to Ajax.

He'll get a laugh out of it. We're always joking about my romantically challenged life.

I check the time in Ajax's world. He'll be sleeping for another two or three hours.

My lips slide up into my first real smile of the night thinking about Ajax sleeping.

I've never actually seen him sleeping, but I imagine he'd wear boxers and a t-shirt and maybe do push-ups right before bed.

Which would explain his beefy arms and broad chest. Not that I've seen those either — well not the chest, but the arms, yes.

I've seen those. I've touched those. Let me tell you, they're spectacular. For a friend, of course.

"BRIDGET!!!" Mrs. Bronowski, my old gym teacher is staring at me while pointing at the dance floor.

"What is it?" I loud whisper back.

"Your sister!"

Before I can ask which one, I hear a cry I know well. I dash across the polished gym floor I once danced the night away on with a tall, handsome Swedish foreign student.

Daisy is standing in the middle of the floor. Her hands cover her face. Tears leak out from between her fingers.

Two of her friends are patting her back and trying to lead her away.

I glance around the room, into the darkest of corners where I made out with boys at dances.

Emerald and Jackson are nowhere to be found.

Chapter Two

BRIDGET

"Why didn't he like me, Bridge, why?"

This right here is why I don't fall in love. I could never let a man reduce me to a puddle of tears. Ever!

I wrap both my arms tightly around my sister's shoulders. Her tear-streaked face is sticky on my neck. I pat her gently. "No boy is worth crying about outside a dance, Daisy. Or crying about anywhere."

She shakes her head in my neck. My dress is probably ruined by her makeup and mascara smudges.

"You don't get it," she hiccups. "You don't love anyone."

Good thing, too, I think.

I murmur, "But I love you. And one day you'll meet someone who loves you for you." That's what I've heard anyway. It's the mantra of hopeless romantics. Which I am not.

My first rule for living a happy life is, "*Don't get attached.*"

I can't tell Daisy that now.

She raises her head and stares at me with deep brown hopeful eyes. "You think I'll meet someone I love as much as I love Jackson? And he'll love me back?"

Before I can answer, she drops her head into my neck with a fresh round of sobs.

My dress is getting wetter by the minute.

I try to remember what I told Ava when she struggled with her romantic meltdown over her boyfriend, Tyler, in Italy. But nothing comes to mind. Because I didn't tell her anything. I did something instead.

At least Ajax, Tyler's best friend, and I did. We took action.

I straighten up and hold Daisy at arm's length. "You know what?"

"What?" she sobs.

"One boy's rejection does not define you. And it sure as hell does not break you. We are going back to that dance."

Daisy shakes her head hard. The beautiful ringlets hanging down her back shimmer with the tinsel that we wove through the curls.

The effect is a romantic moonlit waterfall. Matched with a simple spring green flowy dress. She looks like a dark maiden from a fairy tale.

"Yes, we are," I say firmly. Nobody is ruining my sister's night. Not on my watch.

And it is my watch since I'm the chaperone.

"Let's go," I pull her toward the bathroom by the football lockers.

The one I used to hang out in when I was a freshman. We'd lost our mom when I was in 8th grade. Freshman year of high school is a blur of rebellion. Until I discovered I could forget everything by spending long days and nights in the drama department.

But enough about me.

"Daisy, sweetheart, why don't you wash your face?"

"Here?" she looks around the tiny bathroom.

"I have your makeup bag, remember? We'll do you up again. It'll be fine."

Daisy turns on the faucet and proceeds to scrub her face clean while I dab makeup off the shoulder and neckline of my favorite slinky, bedazzled dress.

I should have worn combat gear for the Jackson meltdown.

After Daisy has wiped away her tears, I brush her chubby cheeks with a little foundation, whisk a little mascara on her eyelashes to highlight her big brown eyes, and for the finishing touch, I swipe glittery lip gloss on her full pouty lips.

I step back and admire my work. "You look . . ."

"What?" her eyes glisten with unshed tears.

"As lovely as always, with or without makeup."

She sniffs. "You're just saying that because you're my sister."

I pull out my phone which is vibrating with messages. I'll get to them later. I snap a photo of Daisy and show her the screen.

"Phones don't lie," I say, screwing up my nose and regretting my statement as soon as it's out of my mouth. Because Jackson sent Daisy many sweet-nothing text messages. Which apparently were all lies.

"You mean mirrors. Like Snow White's stepmother's mirror."

"Yeah, that too."

Daisy giggles. "You're always so . . ."

"Funny? Cool?"

"I was going to say courageous. I wish I had half your courage." Daisy wrings her hands together. "I don't know if I can go back out there, Bridge. I'm not brave like you."

"Hey, I'm not always brave. I'm human." If she only knew how often I cried my eyes out in this very bathroom.

"What's your secret?"

"To not caring what anyone thinks?"

Daisy nods solemnly holding to my hand like she's five instead of eighteen.

"Hmmm."

My phone vibrates again. I glance down and my lips lift in a happy smile. He's up! He must have read my panicky text messages. Although it's only 5 a.m. his time.

"Right. See that look on your face. I want that look," Daisy turns me around to face the mirror.

My dark hair frames my face, flowing in corkscrew curls to my shoulders. My heart-shaped face is glowing, and my eyes are bright. I don't look half bad.

I grin at Daisy.

"It's because of Ajax, isn't it? You only look this way when you're chatting with him."

"I do not."

She nods so hard her ringlets tumble forward. "You do."

I can't deny my excitement that Ajax is texting me all the way from Greece. And that soon I'll be home lying in my bed, looking at his drop-dead gorgeous face and we'll be rehashing everything about my night and discussing his upcoming day.

Since meeting in Italy through Ava and Tyler, we've become . . . well, friends. I'd even say, *best* friends.

"I want that sparkling, cool look."

I burst out laughing and pull Daisy close for a last hug.

"The secret is not taking anything too seriously."

"Why not?"

"Because . . ." I stop. I can't tell her how I had to rebuild myself after Mom passed and I started by making sure I would never get hurt again. Acting on stage was the key for me. But I can't bring up our mother. Daisy was only seven when she died.

No need to remind her that Mom is the one who should be here chaperoning her and Emerald's Spring Fling. Not me. I'm a poor, poor substitute.

Daisy's watching me closely, waiting for my answer.

"Because you gotta believe . . . you gotta know . . . you're amazing. Anything else is icing on the cake and not serious. So, whether

Jackson wants to be your boyfriend is not serious because you're amazing all by yourself."

I can hear myself rambling in my head, so I stop. My words sound empty. They come across as a useless placebo, but hey, I'm reaching here.

She frowns. "Everyone knows you must believe in yourself. We hear that every day. They just don't tell us how!"

I let out a loud sigh. "I wish I knew, kiddo."

Daisy's shoulders slump as does the hopeful expression on her face.

I knew I'd make a lousy chaperone, and Daisy proves I'm right.

We've walked back inside the gym, and Justin Bieber is hogging the soundwaves.

"Do you want to dance or not?" I'm in a tizzy to get on my phone and chat with Ajax, but he'll have to wait.

"Are chaperones allowed to dance?"

"I don't know but I'm going to dance with you," I smirk.

Daisy's eyes shine brightly. "You'll dance with me? For real?" Her eyes target Jackson and Emerald dancing together out on the gym floor.

Emerald is laughing like they're the only couple in the room.

I cringe for Daisy's sake.

"Can we dance right next to *them*?" Daisy eyeballs them hard.

I shake my head at her. "You're a little troublemaker, aren't you?"

She grins. "Thanks for calling me little."

"Your sense of humor," I say.

"What?"

"That's your secret weapon."

"It is?"

I nod firmly. "Your talent for writing, your sense of humor, your kindness to all your sisters, and your love for Freckles, your annoying cat. Those are your winning qualities. They are what makes you amazing. Believe in them."

Her eyes tear up. But this time it's not because of some arrogant bad boy who has the nerve to like two girls at once.

"Come on, sis." I grab Daisy's hand and spin her in a circle. "Let's do this."

Daisy and I execute the Alphabet sisters' dance routine, slapping hands, spinning, and slinking our shoulders together then backward, then dipping and sliding. We're giggling and having so much fun that other kids jump over to our spot and begin following our movements.

I step out of the line of dancers when I see Daisy enjoying herself, showing others the moves that we perfected during long winter evenings.

It doesn't escape me that I'm standing in the circle where the b-ballers jump up to start the game.

I was always good at starting a game. Ask anyone who went to school with me. "She's a player," they said. "She'll play games with you."

The truth was . . . is . . . you'll never catch me crying over a dude. Because as everyone knows, "Bridget Walker doesn't do relationships."

Chapter Three

BRIDGET

By midnight, I still haven't spoken to Ajax. Normally we video chat at midnight, which is seven in the morning for him.

I would snuggle under my covers in PJs and watch him go about his early morning routine with his olive trees. I'm learning a lot about olives. But it's also a nice way to fall asleep.

Hearing Ajax's voice is how I imagine hearing ocean waves breaking on the sand is for many people. Soothing, relaxing, and most of all comforting.

Now, because of Spring Fling, Daisy, Emerald, and I don't arrive back home until after 1 a.m. Dad is out on a date with Maxine, his first-ever girlfriend since Mom, so I'm the parent tonight.

I sit on the sofa and twist Daisy's locks into a silk bonnet so she can sleep without making a tangled mess of her hair. With luck, her hairstyle will last the rest of the week.

"Thanks, Bridge." Daisy hugs me with one arm. Her other arm

is occupied with Freckles clinging to her like a stripey orange purse. I swear that cat has abandonment issues.

"No problem, sweetie."

Then I trudge up the stairs to Emerald's bedroom. With Ava in Italy and Corrine at college, we each get to have our own bedroom.

"Hey Emmie," I call out, knocking lightly on the door. "Can I come in?"

Emerald is the baby in the family. She was only six when Mom died, and she took it the hardest. Although I don't think there was a contest.

Emerald developed paralyzing anxiety. She used to take medication for it, but now she's thriving in high school.

We all believe it's because of her focus on the environment, especially climate change, and her fight to persuade institutions to commit to net-zero greenhouse gas emissions by 2050.

I've learned more about the importance of trees from her and Ajax than I ever thought possible.

Climate change issues still occupy Emerald, but not entirely. Not since Jackson Banza came along.

Ava and Corrine are worried that Jackson may distract Emmie and cause her anxiety to return. They don't want a boy derailing Emerald's progress in any way. I think they're underestimating our baby sister.

Emerald comes out of her bathroom and leaps onto her bed, stuffing her feet under the covers and plopping back onto her ruffled pillow shams.

"Oh Bridget, did you see him? Isn't he gorgeous?" I do my best not to roll my eyes.

My job as the sister in charge is to uplift and support the younger ones. That's what Ava makes clear in her no-nonsense voice when we chat.

I sit on the edge of Emmie's bed and pat her blanketed feet. "Yes, I saw you having a good time with Jackson."

She clutches her hands to her chest like she's Cinderella about to break into song.

"He picked me. I always knew he and I were meant to be. We have a lot in common. He's serious about helping with the Youth Sustainability Leadership Group. And he has a lot of great ideas to help."

I nod and make a noise in my throat that I hope doesn't sound discouraging.

The only idea Jackson has is how to take advantage of Emerald's sweet, innocent demeanor. I know boys like him. Their currency is their charm.

Emerald pops straight up. "You don't like him? Do you? He said you wouldn't. Because of Daisy. But I can't help it if he chose me over her."

"How would you have felt if he chose Daisy instead?"

Her eyebrows slide into a V. "Horrible. But that wasn't going to happen. So do you like him or not?"

I've never been able to lie to any of my sisters. I shake my head. "I don't know him yet."

But I plan to get to know that sucker, better believe it.

Emerald sticks out her bottom lip. It used to be cute when she was little up until she was ten. Now it's a sign she's plotting how to get her way.

Ava and I spoiled her a lot when she was little. But what can you do when your six-year-old sister loses her mother and grows so fearful she can hardly breathe?

You coddle her, that's what you do. I'm not ashamed of it. Except now, it's a disaster. She manipulates us like a sculptor with clay.

Maybe Emerald will manipulate Jackson, and I'll be thinking of him as "poor Jackson" instead.

Secretly, I'm glad Daisy got away from Jackson's clutches. She'd never have survived him.

But Emerald . . . Emerald is no softie. She's a survivor. Whatever Jackson is up to, I bet Emmie can handle it.

We all need to stop worrying about her so much. She's working to save the planet. She's not someone to mess with.

"You'll get to know him soon. He's coming over this weekend."

My head pops up. "What?"

She sighs. "I miss Ava. She'd have baked cookies or done something nice and welcoming for Jackson."

Psshhhht!

If she thinks she can get me to bake cookies for that teenage Casanova, well . . . she's hinting at the wrong sister.

I can't wait to get to my room to call Ajax. To see his smile. Hear his voice. And tell him about this stressful night.

Chapter Four

BRIDGET

Ajax's smiling face peers out at me from my phone. Olive branches seem to be growing out of his head.

"Are you up in a tree? Please don't fall."

The scene swivels upside down and I see thick muscled shoulders, bronzed from the sun, and covered with a film of perspiration.

"Dude! Why are you so sweaty?"

He swipes an arm over his damp forehead. Drops of water drip down his chiseled cheekbones.

"Ewww! Get a towel."

He grins. "You love seeing me hard at work while you lay about in your nightgown."

"I don't wear nightgowns."

"Even better."

I flop back on my bed, laughing at nothing. Well, laughing at the fact I get to speak to this kooky guy every day.

Some days, like today when he's shirtless and the sun is glinting off his sleek muscles, I get a little speechless. Is he for real?

Then I remind myself.

This is Ajax. I refuse to be blinded by his physique. His good looks will never interfere with our friendship.

We're solid. Besties from afar.

He tells me to hold on while he climbs down the ladder that's leaning against a tree.

His phone is clenched between his teeth. I watch his descent.

"That doesn't look safe," I shout.

The ground whips up to greet my face and I scream.

"Did you just jump off the ladder?"

Phone back in hand, Ajax is staring at me, a wide grin splitting his face.

The breath whooshes out of my entire body.

I recognized his Greek god good looks the first day I met him in Italy when I was visiting Ava and he was visiting Tyler.

Over the last six months of video-calling, that vision hasn't lessened. I'm still blown away by his stunning beauty.

Right now, his dark curly hair is plastered to his neck. I watch as he ties a bandana around his head to soak up sweat and unintentionally creates a fierce pirate persona.

I almost laugh. Ajax is so not pirate material. That would be me.

He plops down on a giant boulder and leans back.

"Okay. Tell me all about your night from hell. You made it sound as if you were being tortured instead of hanging out at a party with your sisters."

I sigh. "You have no idea! But I'd rather forget about it now. Can we talk about olives instead?"

He chuckles. "We could. What would you like to know?"

I slide down further under my covers and lean the phone against my pillow. "Oh, tell me about when it's harvest season."

He laughs hard. "I've told you that so many times."

"I know." I smile sleepily. "It's my favorite story about olives."

"Okay," he looks at me with genuine appreciation in his eyes. "Are you ready?"

I almost, but don't, swoon. That would be pointless.

"I'm ready."

Ajax starts recounting how every October they prepare their olive trees for harvest. They place large black nets around the base of the trees and spread them wide as if catching fish.

"But you're catching olives," I say sleepily, my eyes closing down.

His voice floats on. "We shake the branches until they send all of their olives tumbling down."

That's the last I hear about olives as I drift off to sleep.

When I wake up. It's Saturday.

My phone is dead. Ajax is gone and I feel suddenly and inexplicably lonely.

Chapter Five

AJAX

The sun is almost always shining on the island of Aegina, like a gift from Athena herself.

When tourists step off the ferry in Aegina town, they walk right into the life of a fishing village.

All along the waterfront, across from the row of bars and restaurants that sit snugly side by side, are tanned and leathery fishermen, untangling their nets as they perch on the sides of their colorful bobbing boats.

It's a sight that tourists photograph often for their social media, hash-tagging the scene as quaint or authentic.

In reality, it's just fishermen selling their wares and fixing their equipment.

The tourists then move on to the gelato carts and pizza shops.

After they've refueled, they walk down the roadway, past the donkeys, the taxis, and the vendors selling Aegina's main products, like pistachios, and olives, and they settle on beach chairs for the rest of the glorious day.

Only some will rent mopeds or quads or a rattling island car and venture out to see the rest of this amazing island.

Our stunning Temple of Aphaia, on a pine-clad hill, gets few visitors even though it is one of the most beautiful and best-preserved temples in all of Greece.

But even those that find their way into the ancient sanctuary don't make it to what I consider to be Aegina's best-kept secret. Hidden not only from visitors but from locals too.

Aegina's ancient olive grove in the valley of Eleonas.

The ancient trees with their twisted wide trunks, look like dancing monuments. They are 400 to 1500 years old.

When I think about what they've survived and their commitment to the earth, I want to be like these trees. Rooted, grounded, and committed to the planet.

They bear fruit on branches raised to the sky as red and yellow wildflowers dance around their feet in the spring breeze.

I love to sit under my favorite ones and meditate on how to help my own olive trees live as long as these. My best ideas to change our farming methods for a more sustainable future have come after sitting amongst these inspiring trees.

I can't tell anyone on Aegina that. Especially not my father. They'd think I am crazy to believe that the trees are speaking to me.

But Bridget loves to hear me talk about olives and the environment. I wish there was a way we could be together in person.

As soon as that thought enters my head, I brush it away. I don't dwell on impossibilities. I'm a realist and the fact is that Bridget has a life far away from mine. I'm just happy we're best friends.

Before I met Bridget, the site of the ancient olive trees was where I'd come when the harvest wasn't meeting expectations, or the weather was ruinous, the marketing a nightmare, or the accounts incomprehensible.

This is where I'd remind myself that the olive trees are as much a part of me as I'm a part of Aegina.

Maybe more so.

I feel as if the ancient olive trees can impart their wisdom to me. Tell me what to do during difficult times.

And right now, the ongoing battle with my father is the most difficult of times.

How can I convince him that my new farming methods are better for the trees in the long run when he's been doing it the same way long before I was born?

How do you convince someone you love that change is good? More than good. It is necessary. Even if it means losing out on immediate profits to focus on more sustainable investments.

I sigh as I sit under the trees, watching the goats munch grass and the lizards dart from rock to rock.

I check my phone. It's almost morning time in Portland, Maine. Almost time to call Bridget. I better head back to the farm.

The WiFi out here is non-existent and I want to see her beautiful smile and her bright eyes and watch her lips pout as she complains about her little sisters who she loves more than anyone in the world.

As I drive my Jeep back to the farm, I let my mind wander away from reality. How would it feel to be someone Bridget Walker loves more than anyone in the world?

Ha! I shake my head as I arrive at the Christos Farms black iron gates.

My inner voice warns, "You'll never find that out. Get your head out of the clouds and get back to business."

"Yes, sir," I answer back to the voice.

I drive towards the house. I mentally stash away my daydreams about an impossible future. Better to focus on what I do have control over.

Helping my father to understand that my plans for an economically, socially, and environmentally sustainable olive farm are worthy of his approval.

More than that, we'll be creating a model that other olive farmers can implement throughout Greece. Doing our part to help save the planet, one tree at a time.

Chapter Six

AJAX

"The trees aren't going to water themselves, you know." My little sister, Elena, leaps off the steps and lands next to me balancing on one foot and then another.

It's another day and Bridget and I have finished our late night/early morning talk.

I shove my phone into my back pocket.

Thank God, Elena didn't catch me staring at Bridget sleeping in her bed thousands of miles away.

But hey, what's a guy to do when the woman he adores drifts off while he's talking about olives?

As if hearing about my beloved olive farming is the most relaxing thing in the world. She's the perfect woman for me.

If she'd get with the program and like me back! Which she won't because Bridget doesn't do relationships!

The number of times she repeats that mantra, it's annoying, while also being downright discouraging.

My heart needs to get with *her* program and move on.

"You talking to Bridget, again?" Elena grins. "Your *fantasy* girl?"

"Hush," I grin back. "She's a friend. Just a friend."

"Right. And that's why my handsome brother, the most eligible bachelor on our island, won't go out with anyone else?"

I frown and walk toward the trees. "Are you planning on helping me?" I change the subject.

Elena hops along next to me. She reaches for my hand and grabs it in her small rough one.

Rough from almost twelve years of digging in the dirt around our olive farm, and toting rocks and bags of organic fertilizer.

Elena is a farm girl, just like I am a farm boy. Our lives revolve around our olive trees and the award-winning organic oil we produce.

I wouldn't want it any other way.

And based on Elena's unflinching devotion to our trees, even naming some of the older ones as if they're family members, which they are in a sense as some are older than Papa and his father and grandfather, it seems neither would Elena.

When we get to where I left off in the middle of a row of trees, Elena opens the computer printout I've handed her.

"Who's next?" I ask.

Elena reads slowly, her lips moving.

I can tell when she's reached the images. Her eyes light up and it's like watching her brain click into action.

I suppress a smile.

After discovering she has dyslexia and doesn't learn the same way I do; I found a computer program that maps our entire olive grove.

The trees are individually labeled — which is how she started naming them — and we track the growth, hydration, soil, roots, and other key factors to make sure the trees are properly irrigated and pruned, and ready for harvest each year.

It wasn't easy. I had to enlist one of my Harvard pals who is a computer genius to code the program.

But Elena loves it. And I can't imagine how we got along without it.

In addition to Elena's program, we also have the GIS computer program that Papa thought was unnecessary and too expensive, but which I finally convinced him to invest in.

It has turned out to be a big time-saver.

"We never needed computers to know our trees," Papa complains often. "Our trees need humans to understand them, not machines."

But even he glances at the printouts sometimes, which Elena explains to him.

"What've we got?" I look up into the green leafy branches of a tree and smile. It's flowering nicely.

Elena points at the printout. "Peacock spot."

I shake my head. "Not again," I groan. "We just . . ."

"And we need to increase our drip irrigation brother. This month is hotter than ever. Papa's gonna complain about you starving the trees of water."

I press my lips together tightly to stop myself from blurting out what I think Papa can do with his old-fashioned ideas.

"We are not starving the trees. We are conserving water and giving them optimal conditions for growth. What're our soil sensors saying?"

Elena peers at the printout of graphs and numbers.

"There you are," booms a heavy voice.

We both swing around to see Papa at the end of the row sitting atop his idling tractor.

A straw hat is perched atop his dark hair. He's trying in vain to block the sun that has browned his skin to a permanent tan. It's still a chore to get him to wear sunblock out here.

"Hey, Papa," Elena sings out. "Where're you going?"

"To join the crew mulching over in the west field."

Elena makes a face.

"What're you doing?" Papa asks as if he doesn't already know since I told him at breakfast that I was following up on the tree reports. And obviously, that's what Elena is also doing.

Elena waves the printout in her hand.

Papa grunts. "They need more water."

"Yes, they do, Papa," Elena says calmly. "And they'll get the right amount. Ajax knows what he's doing."

I smother a tiny grin. Elena has been my champion ever since the big quarrel occurred after our harvest last November.

It was right after that argument that I dashed off to Florence to visit Tyler, my closest friend.

I had to get away from the farm for a bit, and from the preposterous suggestion Papa had about selling part of our heritage due to low yields because I'd implemented sustainable practices.

That wasn't happening. I insisted he needed to be patient. He shouted that patience didn't pay the bills.

In a way, if Papa and I hadn't had that huge fight, I'd never have gone to Florence and met Bridget. The love of my life.

I push up the wayward curls falling onto my face. Wait! I can't be thinking of Bridget like that. Geez! Friend! Just a friend!

"Yo, bro, Papa is talking to you."

I snap up my head. "Yes, sir?"

"Family meeting tonight."

My heart drops. Our last family meeting was a total disaster.

Even if it reaped some positive results . . . like meeting Bridget.

"Yes sir," I growl.

Papa rides off toward the west field and Elena hands me the computer printout.

"Is everything going to be okay?" Elena's voice shakes. "With the farm?"

"Of course," I say automatically.

"Ajax?" her voice is low. "You can tell me the truth."

I heave out a big breath. Look her in the eye. "We're going to make sure Christos Farms is just fine."

Elena pats the gray knotty trunk of the tree we're checking out. "He's family."

I slide my hand over the rough tree trunk. The hard surface feels solid, real, and permanent.

Not a lot of things in this world feel like a strong, sturdy olive tree. The symbol of peace, wisdom, and prosperity.

Or as Homer called olive oil, "liquid gold."

I turn to Elena. "We are growing the liquid gold of the gods. We will not fail."

Her smile is hesitant. "Promise?"

I roll my eyes at her and she giggles.

But inside my head, I'm making crazy promises to her, to myself, to our nonni who built this farm.

"Cool." Her smile lights up her face.

"Cool."

I study the computer printout.

After only one year of harvests with the newly implemented methods, our olive oil yield is smaller. Papa wants to give up and go back to the old ways.

I have to stay the course. I have to keep believing that what I'm doing is right for the farm. To protect its delicious and precious olive oil. And protect the environment.

I gaze around as far as I can see. Olive trees wave their branches as if they're cheering me on.

They've been a part of my life for twenty-six years. Mama would spread my baby blanket under the shady trees and leave me to gaze upwards into their crowns. I've seen plenty of baby pictures of me staring at the trees.

Mama said my first word was "tree."

I feel them breathing. And hear them talking to each other. Their tree voices are whispers in the wind.

I'm not selling any part of Christos Farm. Not now. Not ever.

Chapter Seven

AJAX

At the family meeting, I sit still with my hands clenched before me listening to my father present the most preposterous idea.

When he's finished, I stare at him and say firmly, "I'm not doing that. I refuse." In my head, I sound like a petulant child. But he's asking for the impossible.

"Ajax, you said you'd do anything to save our farm."

"You want me to marry a stranger to save it? Are you both crazy?" I eye Mama, begging her to see that Papa is not making any sense.

Elena, who insisted on attending the family meeting now that she's almost a teenager, sits with her hands clasped over her mouth. Like she's trying not to blurt out anything inappropriate.

"Mama?" I stare hard at my mother.

She holds up both hands in a surrendering gesture. "I agree with your father."

Elena lets out a squeak.

Mama shuts her down with a look.

"No, let Elena speak," I say.

Elena drops her hands and stabs me in the back with her traitorous words. "Sorry, bro, but you're not getting any younger."

I give her the evil eye.

She shrugs and goes back to covering her mouth with her hands.

Papa pushes back his chair and stands. "Son, arranged marriages are normal. People all over the world do it. I did it!" His voice has not yet reached volcanic levels, so I'm thinking I can still talk some sense into him.

I glance at Mama. She nods. I'd heard their story before, but I don't remember the details. And frankly, it seemed like such an ancient practice. Nothing relevant for me in the 21st century.

I press my lips together so I don't blurt out what's blaring in my head. *You all are nuts!*

That doesn't stop the balloon of fear rising to my throat. My heartbeat races like when I was running in the round-the-island marathon. Nothing felt worse than that breathless, dizzy feeling of my lungs almost collapsing.

Until this.

"You aren't really asking me to marry a stranger?" I half-whisper, my lungs barely giving me the oxygen I need to stand up to my parents.

"That's the thing! You already know the girl. She's not a stranger." Dad's hand smacks the polished tabletop with a loud *whoomp*. Like he'd been waiting to pull out this trump card.

I blink.

Elena drops her hands. "I'm going to get a sister?" She beams.

"You're not," I rumble, ready to defend my right to choose my own bride. One day. One faraway day.

But when I turn to Mama and Papa, I feel like I'm ten years old again. I struggle to find my voice. "Who is she?"

Before either of them can answer, I add, "I don't know any

single woman on Aegina that I would marry. Or who would want to marry me."

Papa scoffs. So do Mama and Elena. I think Mama even rolls her eyes.

"Well?" I ask.

"Iona Galanis."

I blink. Hard. "Are you out of your mind? She hates me."

Papa waves his hand in the air like that's not a good enough reason to not marry someone.

"And we haven't seen each other since high school. That was . . ." I look up at the ceiling and count in my head, "almost eight years ago! I went away to college, and she disappeared. I haven't seen her since."

"Well, she's very wealthy now . . . she also went away to college and is doing something with banks in Japan. I ran into her father at their taverna in town. And guess what?"

"What?" we all ask him, although my "what" comes out like *WHAT*?

Papa looks around the table, his face splitting into a rare smile. It almost makes me smile back. But nope.

He puts his hands together like he's praying.

"Ajax Achilles Christos," he says using my full name, which scares me more than anything. When your Greek father calls up the ancient warriors you're named after, you know a big ask is coming.

"You are my only son. You are the heir to the Christos Farms and Olive Oil Company."

A loud ahem from my little sister stops him for a moment. "Yes, you too, dear," he says with a wink at her.

"I'm afraid our olive oil is not selling like it once did. The market is down. Your new-fangled ideas are ruining us. We're making much less money since we're selling fewer bottles."

"But Papa," I interrupt. "As olive farmers, our water usage and carbon footprint . . ." I stop when I see his eyes rolling upwards.

"Okay, let me be clear. If we don't change the way we farm and make oil, the scorching temperatures hitting us during the summers due to climate shifts will cause a loss of crops. In less than ten years we could lose everything. It's essential that we implement these new methods of farming."

Papa crosses his arms and stares at me as if I am Death himself.

"Sorry," I soften my tone, "to be the bearer of this harsh news, but I've been telling you this for years."

Mama taps her fingernails on the wooden table. Elena bites her bottom lip, looking distressed. Papa flicks his eyes toward me, holding me in his gaze.

"Those are speculations, Ajax," Mama says. "Right now, we're paying off the loans for the new farm equipment. And the fancy new bottles you insisted we order."

Papa nods. "And the new computer equipment and whatever that satellite thing is that we pay to oversee our trees from *space*!"

I raise my hand to interrupt to explain for the hundredth time how all of this will help us in the long run. He shushes me.

"Not to mention the cost of putting in that new irrigation drip system to save water, and give our trees just sips when they need gulps!"

"We're conserving water, Papa."

He shrugs. "Okay, but I have compromised on so much, don't you think?"

I watch him warily. "Yes, you have," I say reluctantly. "Thank you for listening to my ideas."

He beams. "Listening and doing your ideas!"

I nod.

"Okay, then it's time for you to listen and do *my* idea. It's called compromise, is it not?"

Oh no. I drop my head in my hands. How has Papa outsmarted me?

Papa can't seem to stop smiling as he continues. "Mister

Galanis and I had a nice long talk about our children. He wants Iona to come back home. Like any good Greek child should do."

I grit my teeth.

"Strange enough, Iona's looking to get into the olive oil business."

"Coincidentally strange," I mutter. I can almost taste blood on my tongue.

"*And* he says, she's ready to settle down. So, I put one and one together . . . and . . ."

"You got four?"

He nods excitedly. Totally missing my sarcasm.

"This is a great opportunity Ajax Achilles Christos. For you. For Iona. For everyone."

"We wouldn't have to sell any part of the family land because she's going to invest in Christos Oil once she's your wife." Papa smiles like he's personally solved global problems.

"Right, you won't sell the land, but you'll sell me," I grumble.

"The best part is," Papa continues, his dark eyebrows rising dramatically into the silver curls on his forehead, "she'll be right here helping you run it so your mama and I can relax a bit. It's what the Americans call a win-win, no?"

Mama reaches over and pats Papa's hand. "Get ready for a big fat Greek wedding, my love."

Elena squeals. "Can I be a bridesmaid? Pretty please! Ajax, can I?"

I stand up and gaze hard at my father. He's much shorter than I am. In my socks, I stand six feet two inches tall, a throwback to my mythological ancestor the Great Ajax, warrior champion, grandson of King Aiakos, the first King of Aegina.

The same Ajax of the Trojan Wars. Cousin to Achilles.

I wish I could call on his courage now to fight my father. Not with swords, of course, but with words and logic. All of which have deserted me.

"You have to marry someone," Mama says, hopefully.

"Yes! Someone who *loves* me. Someone I love, too." I blurt.

Papa snorts. "Love is a verb. You will learn to love."

My eyes open wide. "Who are you, Oprah?"

Papa and Mama laugh merrily.

I can't believe my family — even my little Elena — is ready to sell me off to the highest bidder to save our olive farm.

I leave the family meeting and head upstairs. There's only one person I want to talk to right now. I glance at my phone. I hope Bridget is near her phone and free to talk, even if she's far across the Atlantic Ocean.

Chapter Eight

AJAX

"They want you to do what?!" Bridget's outrage is reassuring.

For the last ten minutes, I've waited for her to drive home from her hair appointment in preparation for a big book launch she's covering this evening in Boston for her job.

I've been pacing up and down my bedroom carpet. I have the largest bedroom in the house. It was constructed recently as an extension with skylights, built-in bookcases, and a huge bathroom.

It's a graduation present, my parents had said, when I returned from college and they wanted me to live on the farm.

Our house is big anyway, but now I have my own private suite. Private studio suite, as it features a sleek kitchenette.

I screw open a bottle of water and collapse on the sofa. If I lean back, I can gaze at the stars popping out in the night sky above my head.

But Bridget's on the video call now looking stunning, her hair a smooth flowing waterfall caressing her face. I love her curly hair, but the sleek look enhances her tilted brown eyes.

The stars are no competition. She has my full attention. She always does.

"No way, Ajax. This isn't the 1800s." Bridget's eyes flash dangerously.

"Well, actually, Bridge, people still have arranged marriages. It's part of many cultures."

"On Netflix, you mean, not in real life!"

I sigh. "My parents don't see it that way."

I explain everything my father said, all the evidence he put forth to back up his request – or his demand. "I'm still not sure what my options are here. Truthfully, I can see my parents' side of it."

"Well, I don't." Bridget's deep brown eyes have widened into saucers. "You have to refuse. They can't make you."

"Maybe I should talk to Iona. See what she thinks. This may all be some crazy plan cooked up by two old men. Maybe she's adamantly against it and I won't have to think about it again."

Bridget crosses her legs and leans forward, her lovely, toned arms resting on her knees as she faces her propped-up phone.

"That could be one solution. But suppose she's on board. Then what?"

We stare into each other's eyes silently.

I notice the little mole by her upper lip. Her forehead is creased in worry for me.

The beautiful, sweet lips that normally are curled into a smile are turned downwards.

"Are you really that close to losing your farm?"

I shrug. "I don't think so. But we've had two years of losses. And Papa is worried about us making it through the next few crops. I am, too. Implementing the new methods was costly, but our extra virgin oil quality is better than before."

"I can't wait to taste the olive oil from Christos Olive Farm. Every time you talk about it, I can almost taste its delicious richness on my tongue. Your Dad's got to agree you've got a high-quality product."

"He does. But the financials aren't adding up. Yet. And may not add up for a while. He says either we sell a piece of our land, or I marry Iona Galanis."

Bridget's mouth forms an O.

"So, you'd be marrying this woman strictly for her money?"

I cover my eyes. "Don't say it like that. It would be a marriage of convenience. Our farm would survive. And she would get into the olive oil business."

"And she'd get you. As her husband," Bridget says, her features screwing up. "What is she like?"

I shudder. "I haven't seen her since we graduated high school. Suppose I'm not attracted to her. Suppose she's not attracted to me?"

Bridget scoffs. "Please, dude, who's not attracted to you?"

I want to say, "You!" But I bite my lip.

Nothing here is going as planned.

I'm not sure how I thought Bridget would help.

I only knew I needed to hear her voice and see her face and I'd calm down.

"Help me think of something fast, okay? Because Iona Galanis didn't like me in high school. She hated me. If she wants to marry me now, it's probably to get revenge."

"The plot thickens," Bridget mutters.

"It's true. She told everyone I had 'imposter syndrome.' I'll never forget that because I didn't know what she meant."

"What did she mean?"

"She said I had to figure it out. Then, in my yearbook, she wrote . . . hold on."

I grab the yearbook off the bottom shelf of my bookcase and flip to the page that I had dog-eared and creased up in the first year after graduation.

I read aloud, "I hope you find your true self one day and stop believing the hype."

A choking sound emanates from Bridget's phone.

"Are you laughing?"

"Dude, what did you do to her?"

I sit back and glance up at the stars, trying to remember my school days on this tiny island where we all knew each other.

Nothing memorable comes to mind.

I shrug. "No idea. But it wasn't big because everyone would have been discussing it, even now. Small island residents don't forget anything."

She taps her slender fingers on her chin, leaning forward even more and almost falling into the phone. "This sounds like a Greek drama in the making."

"No! Help me put a stop to it. Please! I don't want to spend the rest of my life regretting saving my farm."

Bridget stands up. "I have to go to work."

"Oh, I'm sorry," I say hurriedly.

She holds up a hand. "No Ajax, it's okay. I'm waiting on Daisy and Emerald to arrive home in one piece before heading out. I have an almost two-hour drive ahead of me. Plenty of time to think up a solution for you."

I hate how sad and desperate I'm coming across. I'm supposed to be a solid guy with the answers to my own life. But I'm feeling as if my world is falling apart.

Bridget must pick up on my mood. Her voice softens.

"Listen, I'm here for you. I owe you for the help you gave me in Italy. Getting Ava and Tyler back together."

I nod absently.

She stares at me as I lean back on the sofa, one hand holding the phone, the other arm thrown over the back of the couch.

What is she seeing when she looks at me? I sure hope it's not a pathetic creature.

"You don't owe me anything, Bridge," I sigh. "But I do need your advice. Help me get out of this mess!"

"Well, it's not a mess yet," she ponders.

"That's not true. They're already planning a big fat Greek wedding."

"Dude, you should have started with that. I'm on it!"

Chapter Nine

BRIDGET

By the time I've closed out of the video call with Ajax, my heart is beating weirdly fast.

Images of Ajax in a tux standing up at an altar saying "I do" to some woman whose face I can't imagine but who I'm sure is stunning, flit through my mind at top speed.

I can't stop the movie from unfolding.

Ajax's tall, rugged body straining against the fabric of a tuxedo not meant to encase such broad shoulders.

His strong, curved lips repeating wedding vows. His bronzed fingers slipping an antique ring onto a woman's delicate fingers.

More vows, then a deep kiss that goes on too long with Ajax wrapping his arms around her smooth shoulders, her gossamer and silk wedding dress hugging her curves in all the right places.

A dress to die for. A dress I would choose for myself.

Then, loud cheers from the crowd of Greeks on Aegina. The entire island has turned out to wish the local couple a happy and prosperous marriage.

Olive branches are waved over their heads as they take their first walk as husband and wife.

I choke on the word, "wife." But the movie doesn't stop.

At the reception, wine overflows from golden chalices once held aloft by their ancestors.

Baklava and other Greek treats are being passed around by handsome waiters.

And then, the camera zooms in on a lone figure in the crowd.

Is that me? In a satin dress, blue as the Greek island sky, blue as my soul and feelings.

Why am I not happy for my best friend?

After a lot of dancing, breaking of plates, spinning, and clapping, Ajax and his bride step into a rowboat moored to the dock.

A fisherman rows them out to a yacht! To start their honeymoon. As the sun sets on this idyllic scene.

"Yo Bridget, what're you doing?"

I jump at the sound of Daisy's voice. She's standing right next to me in the kitchen. I didn't see or hear her come in, that's how lost I was in my daydream of Ajax's wedding.

"What's wrong with you?" she asks. "You look like you lost your best friend."

I gulp.

She stops on her way toward the stairs. Her backpack sits squarely on her back bulging with books.

Freckles has draped his supersized body across her chest. She's nuzzling him asking if he had a good day. He purrs a mile a minute.

"Um . . ." I glance at the clock above the counter. "I have to go. I've got an event at seven o'clock in Boston. But I'll be back by eleven. Midnight at the latest. You guys know what to do. Homework, dinner, no boys."

Daisy's face, buried in orange stripey fur, emerges with a frown. "Right, no boys, I got that memo a while ago."

"Sorry."

"What are you so deep in thought over anyway? Is everything okay?" She's talking to me but looking at Freckles.

I stuff beauty products in my bag, along with my phone, portable tripod, and phone light.

I sigh. "Not really."

I wonder if I should confide in Daisy. Usually, I wouldn't hesitate to tell Ava. But Ava's not returning from Italy for another couple of weeks.

"You can share with me," Daisy says, picking up on my hesitation. "Sisterly advice can go both ways."

I smile at her. "You're right." I glance at the clock again. "Where's Emerald?"

At that moment the front door swings open and Emmie rushes in. She's texting and walking and I'm afraid she'll fall over.

"Slow down, baby girl."

She rewards me with a big smile. She waves to Daisy and then heads upstairs, her thumbs still flying on her phone.

"Homework, Emerald Walker, then dinner and no BOYS!" I shout after her, but I don't think she hears me.

Daisy looks at me and rolls her eyes. "I'll make sure *she* gets the memo."

"Please, and thank you."

"So, what's your problem?"

Freckles and Daisy both look at me with cute round faces and sweet eyes.

"Ajax is getting married."

The moment the words leave my lips, my heart deflates. Like a balloon has been popped.

I can almost feel my entire body deflating along with my heart.

Daisy drops her arms and Freckles leaps to the floor.

"No way!" Daisy cries, rushing to my side. "No, no, how is that possible?"

"Are you crying?" I ask Daisy, shocked to see water gathering in her eyes.

"Of course, I am, why aren't you?"

"Um . . . because we're friends? I don't like Ajax in a romantic way. Why should I be concerned that he *may* be getting married?"

Yet, I seem to be a lot more than concerned. Jitters are making my hands sweat and my lips dry. None of this makes sense.

Daisy throws her arms around me. "You're in denial, sis. Ajax is your one true love!"

"Stop being dramatic. He is not."

Daisy sniffs and leans back to look me in the eyes. For unknown reasons, I can't meet hers.

"Anyway, it's an arranged marriage. He wants to get out of it."

Daisy's face lights up as if I said he's Greece's Crown Prince. Daisy is all about royalty and old-fashioned courtship. She must have watched *Bridgerton* ten times.

"What are we gonna do to stop this travesty? Hijack the groom? Bust up the nuptials? Tell me!" Daisy's face takes on a worrying excitement.

I shake my head at my sister's overactive imagination. "This is not a rom-com. This is serious stuff. He's miserable."

Daisy holds open her hands. "Well then, there's only one thing to do."

"What?" I ask, heading toward the front door. I have to get out of here or I'll be late.

"You must go to Greece. You must see for yourself if you and Ajax are meant to be together. Before he accidentally marries the wrong woman, and three lives are ruined."

"Are you out of your mind!?" I ask, almost crashing into the glass on the inside of the door.

"Bridget Walker, I may not know much about boys. But I know a lot about you. And you've been glowy and smiley since meeting him. If you don't go, you may regret it forever."

I blink. "I hate to tell you this, Daisy, but I'll have to take the chance of regretting it forever. Because the last thing I'm doing is getting on a twelve-hour flight to chase a man. Don't you know *that* about me?"

Daisy shakes her head sadly. "Stubborn is not your best look."

I slam the door on my way out. It doesn't feel as satisfying as I thought it would.

Chapter Ten

BRIDGET

Despite all my worrying thoughts about Ajax and his prospective arranged marriage, I've managed to drive onto the I-95 South ahead of any rush hour traffic.

The highway is clear. The sun is a glowing ball in the sky, just starting its westward slide.

Our warmer weather has pushed up an abundance of spring flowers. They wave their colorful heads along the side of the highway.

I cast my eyes to the horizon trying to forget Daisy's words.

She's wrong. I'm Bridget Walker. I don't get attached to any guy. I don't do relationships. Even with a gem like Ajax.

My phone buzzes and it's the coordinator of the book launch asking what my ETA is.

I tell her what time I expect to arrive based on my GPS and pray there's no traffic when I hit the Boston loop.

Focus, Bridge. Focus on Boston. Think about the excitement of being back in the city of champions.

With its Museum of Fine Arts, its theaters, and clubs, and the large green Boston Common that features outdoor Shakespeare performances. Even if I don't perform anymore, I love being in the audience.

Ajax asked me once why I stopped acting. I said it was because I had to help take care of my baby sisters. It was too time-consuming.

Oh, great, my thoughts have made their way back to Ajax.

As usual.

The tornado of emotions swirling through my head and heart at the idea of him marrying someone else won't die down.

As I hurtle down the highway to Boston, I force myself to put Ajax out of my mind.

Tonight will be exciting. I love the city. I'll meet new people. Maybe make new friends.

I'll hear a famous author talk about her book. I'll take photos of the famous author for the publisher's social media platforms. I'll think of creative ways to use the content.

Yes, Bridget. This is your life. You have a career. Of sorts. You have your family. You have lots of friends. Thousands of them — just check your IG and TikTok.

Nothing's missing. Well . . . I slam the brakes on my internal dialogue. That's not true.

Mom is missing. She's always missing. Every single time I took to the stage to perform, Mom was missing in the front row.

When anything exciting happens, or even a not-so-exciting thing, just an ordinary event, I want to run home and tell her.

Thirteen was the worst age possible for losing my mother.

With my period coming, my breasts growing, my braces coming off, and most of all, my heart falling into an icy pond freezing from the outside in.

I can't tell anyone. Not Dad or my sisters, not Ajax or my friends. No one. But I feel as if my heart is stuck in that pond. It's frozen solid, sunk to the bottom and I can't retrieve it.

That spot under the rib cage where everyone has a heart — I have a hollowed space.

Over the years, I've accepted myself as I am. I've accepted that I'm incapable of falling in love. No matter how much I may want to commit, my heart does not cooperate.

It's as if it already knows there'll be a painful outcome and it doesn't want to go there. So, yeah, me and happy ever after with a man — not happening.

Which is exactly why I need to focus on my career. At least this way I have some control. And my heart doesn't have to take a deep dive into misery. Because I'm not letting any man break it. It's called self-care.

THE BOOKSHOP IS DECORATED IN SUNSET COLORS TO match the title and theme of the author's book, *Sailing into the Sunset Years of Life.*

It's not a book I'd usually pick up and read. But now that I'm here, I peek at the chapter headings and flip through the pages as I wait for the audience to be seated.

The book has chapters like, "Be Fearless" and "New Skin in the Game," which I find intriguing.

In between taking shots on my camera phone, I start reading the book.

I get so engrossed that I miss the introduction of the famous author.

I spend the next hour stooping down in between rows of readers, standing on a high chair in the back, and even scooting along the floor in my nice pants and sweater to get the perfect shots.

Afterward, the bookstore owner comes over and introduces herself. She asks to be tagged on the posts. I assure her I'll tag her, and she goes off with a big smile. She'll get free publicity for days out of this.

It's when I'm packing up my tripod and rolling up the tiny mic's wires, that the author comes over to my side.

It's not unusual.

Some authors want the photos sent to them for pre-approval.

But this author doesn't say a word.

There's something eerie about her. Intense and eerie.

"Hi, Bridget," she says. Although she's in her late 70s, her voice is clear as a bell.

I'm wearing a lanyard with my name on it, so I'm not shocked she knows my name.

"Hi, Ms. Berry. You were wonderful."

"Thank you. You made it fun watching you try to concentrate on my reading and the Q&A while your mind was a million miles away."

I drop the mic and the wires unravel. "Shoot." I pick it up, my hands shaking.

"What do you mean?"

She smiles mysteriously. "You were reading my book."

I nod, swallow, and nod again. "I hope that's okay."

"Of course. But why? You're in your sunrise years. Not your sunset ones."

I frown. I can't tell this stranger my sunrise years ended when I was thirteen. The hollow feeling in my chest is a constant reminder I'm living more of a sunset life where possibilities are limited.

The author sits down in the empty seat next to where I'm packing up my bag.

"What's on your mind?"

I feel my face heating up. "Nothing."

She smiles, wrinkles papering her cheeks and eyes, like the cover of a favorite book you've read over and over. "You can tell me. Maybe I can help. In any case, I'm not going to see you again. So it's safe with me."

I smile. "You're very kind. It's about a friend."

She sighs. "No, it's not. It's about you. Everything is about us, no matter how much we think it's not."

"What . . . do . . . you mean?" I stammer.

She picks up the copy of the book I was reading. I plan on paying for it before I leave the store.

She opens it up and scribbles a message, signs her name with a flourish, and shuts the book firmly like she's closing a treasure chest.

"Here. You must allow the sun to go down so you can welcome it when it rises again. And it *will* rise again. It always does."

I frown. "What do you mean?'

She smiles that papery smile. "Just an old lady's musings. You look like you're holding onto a sunset. Not letting it go down. You're going to miss a lot of sunrises if you continue like that."

I stare after her as she walks away. Cane in hand, her shuffle belying the sharp quick eyes she turns back to look at me with.

"Bridget Walker, don't forget," she says, in her clear-as-a-bell voice. "The sun rises every day, even when it's cloudy or rainy. Can you do the same?"

I frown at her back as she sashays off, cane and all.

Why does it feel like she was speaking on behalf of my mother?

Chapter Eleven

BRIDGET

The lights in the kitchen are on when I arrive home. A plate of freshly baked cookies sits atop the counter.

A handwritten note in a purple pen is splayed open so I won't miss it. I smile as I peer at Daisy's curlicues.

Dear Bridget,
These cookies are sweet
but I'm feeling blue
If you don't love Ajax
I'll be miserable for you.

I laugh aloud and bite into one of Daisy's famous chocolate chip delights. I hate to disappoint her fairy tale idea of true love. But me and Ajax?

No way!

She should know better after her heartbreaking dip in the falling-in-love pool with Jackson.

You don't always get what you want. Even if I wanted to be with Ajax, there are too many obstacles keeping us apart.

I live in Portland, Maine. He lives on a Greek island in the Saronic Gulf.

I am a big-city content creator who needs fiber optics. He lives on an olive farm and needs . . . water?

I love shoes and concerts, bookstores, and being close to my sisters.

He loves olive trees, sunshine, rain, and fertilizers. And being close to *his* family.

We are complete opposites. And as incompatible as . . . well, J. Lo and everyone she dates.

Okay, that's mean. She's back with Ben Affleck after a twenty-year hiatus.

Maybe in twenty years Ajax and I will run into each other somewhere and fall in love.

But right now, it's an impossible situation.

Chapter Twelve

BRIDGET

I take a longer shower than usual because I'm trying to decide whether to call Ajax. There haven't been many nights when I don't call him before going to sleep.

If I don't call tonight, it might send the wrong message.

He needs my advice.

But I'm flooded with contrary messages from my heart. From Daisy. Even from Ms. Berry, the author. I don't want to inadvertently blurt out anything weird to him.

It could ruin our relationship. Our friendship, I mean.

It doesn't matter anyway, because my phone is vibrating madly on my bed when I walk in.

I throw on a clean tank top and undies and dive under the covers.

I slide open my phone and break into a natural smile when I see his face.

He's staring at his phone with a murderous expression.

"Ajax!"

Instantly, a giant smile lights up his face. "Bridget!"

That chunk of ice I call my heart that's stuck on the bottom of a frozen pond cracks a tiny bit.

We're two silly kids grinning at each other.

"I missed you." He's staring so hard at me that I have to look away.

"I'm right here." I try to stay nonchalant on the outside. But I can't help the backflips going on inside my stomach.

"Any new developments on your end?" I ask. "Did you get a chance to talk to Iona?"

He shakes his head. "Not yet. Later today."

I breathe out in relief. It's not too late.

"I want you to know I'd marry you myself if I had the money. To help save your family's farm. I just want to put that out there."

It's only after I've said it that I realize I could have just said I'd give him the money. Not that I'd marry him!

He'd been looking down as I spoke. Now, his head pops up.

I stare at his soulful dark, almost black eyes. The truth is, I wish we could date. And fall in love.

But there are too many obstacles between us. Not to mention my traitorous heart.

I don't want to ruin our friendship by taking that kind of chance.

"I'd marry you, too," he says despondently as if he knows it could *never* happen!

"In a heartbeat," he adds trying to smile.

I blink once. Twice. An insane idea forming in my head.

"Well then, why don't we tell your family that?"

What the heck am I saying?

Ajax freezes. When he opens his mouth to speak, he struggles to wrap his tongue around the words. "Tell them what?"

Out of the blue, or maybe out of the fantasy Daisy's planted in my head, I blurt out, "That *we* are engaged."

My phone screen goes black. I hear a scuffling noise.

"Ajax?"

His gorgeous face reappears.

"I lost you for a moment." He pauses. "My phone fell out of my hand. I'm not sure I heard correctly. I don't understand."

That makes two of us buddy.

But I stifle any doubts and try to do what that wise author of self-help books said.

I try to make room for a new sunrise in my life. I glance at my bedside clock. Even if it's after midnight.

"If you don't want to marry the woman they've chosen for you, then tell your family you've already asked another woman to be your wife. Tell them you're an engaged man. They can't expect you to marry Iona Galanis if you're in love with someone else, right?"

My screen goes dark again.

"Are you there?"

When he reappears, he's standing outside. Next to his beloved olive trees.

I was only seeing his face before, but now with the way he's holding the phone, I can see more of him.

His golden bare chest with pecs the size of bricks.

His chiseled hip V lines jutting out above the waistband of his pants.

"Seriously!"

"What's wrong?"

I shake my head in exasperation. He's a fricking Greek god! And he's kind and thoughtful and a great listener. He can marry anyone.

"Bridget Walker, what exactly do you mean I should tell my family I'm already engaged? Is this a joke to you? My future isn't a joke."

His dark eyes glisten through the screen. I reach out a hand to try and touch him. Which is impossible.

"I'm saying, you idiot, that I'm coming to your rescue. Will you, Ajax Achilles Christos, of Aegina, marry me?"

Total silence.

My stomach does Simone Biles somersaults.

His facial muscles are moving funny. Stretching wide and up as dimples appear. Is he smiling? Frowning? Crying?

"We'll be fake fiancés," I hurry up and clarify before he thinks I'm crazy. "You know I don't commit."

His face settles into an expression that looks like disappointment.

"I'm sorry this is the best I can come up with. To help you out. We can buy you time to improve the farm profits. And I'll help you with that, too."

"How?"

My mind is zinging all over the place. "I'm a marketer. I can help."

He frowns.

"Yes . . . I can help you recharge your product line. Develop a more connected social media presence." My words are flowing faster than my brain cells. How am I going to do all that? I've never tasted the oil. Or seen the farm.

"We don't have a social media presence. We have a website," he grumbles.

I can feel my eyes growing wide.

"Christos Olive Farms is leaving a lot of money on the table. Do you realize how much income you can generate with a presence to attract global customers?"

He shakes his dark curls. But I have his full attention. I slide up the strap of my tank top that keeps slipping down.

"You have a supreme organic product, grown in a super sustainable manner, so people worldwide will love you."

A silver light blooms on his face. "That's what I've been telling Papa! Our olive grove is a carbon dioxide sink. Our trees remove CO2 from the atmosphere and fix it in the soil."

I nod vigorously. How many times have I listened to Ajax tell me about his olive forest, and how all the changes he's added are an important part of the solution to climate change. I know it intimately.

I jump up on my knees. My hair flies behind me. "This is perfect, Ajax. You'll have loyal customers pouring in to support your efforts. You're not just selling a product — you're packaging hope for the future."

"Whoa!"

I giggle. We're staring into each other's eyes. I don't know what he's thinking, but I'm thinking this could work.

"What's in it for you?" he asks suddenly. "You can't just sacrifice your single status for nothing. Even if it's fake."

He stutters on the last word.

I think about it for a few seconds.

Finally, I say, "Um . . . a trip to Greece this summer? I've always wanted to see Aegina. And we'll have to show your parents you're serious. Not just about us, but the way we'll save the farm by rebranding your olive oil. And Ava and Tyler are returning home, so I have the entire summer to get away. Trust me I need a break."

I omit how the "us" part of the equation isn't serious at all.

"You want to come to Greece?" His voice rises in pitch.

I nod. A smile escapes my lips. "I want to see you again. Is that okay?"

I don't usually sound so insecure and needy. But my empty rib cage has been giving off emergency signals since talking to Ms. Berry about life. Maybe I need to take some chances. Why not start with this?

If I'm being honest, I'm tired of talking to him by phone. I want to hear his laugh for real and touch his arm as we speak long into the night. I want to be there for him . . . *as a friend*.

"Oh my, Bridge, I'd love for you to come here. I have so much to show you. You'll love Aegina. The food, the wine, the beaches . . ."

"The olive oil," I interject.

We end our conversation with a lot of laughter practicing our sweet goodnights now that we're officially fake fiancés.

I haven't laughed so much in a long time. Ajax insists we need pet nicknames. We end by agreeing to come up with a name for each other.

It feels good to see Ajax happy and smiling again.

Later, as I'm tossing and turning to try and sleep, worry sets in.

What am I getting myself into? Will I ruin Ajax's farm if our plan doesn't work out?

Will I ruin my and Ajax's friendship if I flake and can't commit even to being a fake girlfriend?

Most of all, will I ruin my strongly preserved position as the Alphabet sister no one can pin down?

Chapter Thirteen

AJAX

All day as I work in the hot sun, I think about Bridget's plan to save me from the arranged marriage, which my parents are getting more excited about.

At lunch, Dad called Mr. Galanis in front of me and Mama to confirm that we'd have dinner at his family's taverna this week. To discuss my and Iona's future.

My heart dropped to my feet. How was I going to break the news of my fake engagement to them now?

Papa looked so happy he was beaming, something I hadn't seen him do in a long time.

And Mama was full of smiles as she handed around plates of hot food. Papa's good mood was rubbing off on everyone.

Even old Zorro's tail was thumping happily on the wooden floor like he sensed there'd be extra bones from extravagant wedding meals in his future.

By the time the sun is going down and the air is getting cooler with cicadas buzzing loudly in the olive trees, I know I have to man up.

Or, as I call it in my head whenever I must do something brave like confront my father, it is time for a Hercules move.

I wait until after dinner. After Papa has eaten and is sipping some wine, tilted back in his chair.

Elena's telling him about a school trip she is going on to see Poseidon's temple in Athens. Mama is clearing the table and watching me with worried eyes.

I'm flipping my fork up and over as if playing quarters back at college. I became supremely good at that game so I wouldn't have to drink the beer in those red plastic cups.

Part of me wishes I was back at school when all I had to worry about were grades and not drinking warm beer.

My phone vibrates. It's a text from Bridget.

I'm waiting until after Daisy's graduation party to tell my family I'm going to Greece for the summer.

She adds her favorite emoji—a monkey covering his face with his hands. *What about you?*

I type fast under the table. *I'm telling them now.* I send her back the same emoji.

I'm there in spirit with you. Be brave, my Hercules.

How does she always know what to say?

I swallow a nervous laugh. Two young adults in our 20s and we're afraid of upsetting our parents.

I wait for Elena to stop talking and clear my throat. "Excuse me, I have to tell you all something."

My family looks at me. Elena with humor on her face. Mama with still worried eyes. And Papa? He closes his eyes and slowly reopens them. Like he knows I'm about to dash his grand plans for a marriage of convenience.

I blink hard. You got this, Ajax, I tell myself.

"I'm afraid I can't marry Iona Galanis."

Papa sighs. "Not this again."

Mama puts a hand on his arm. "Let's hear what Ajax has to say."

I press my lips together hard. Formulate the words in my head. I look from one family member to the next, willing them to believe what I'm going to say.

Elena ducks her head to look at me, sympathy in her eyes. "You seem nervous."

I focus my mind on Bridget coming to Greece. Being in Aegina next to me. It's the only thing giving me the courage to lie to my family now. Although it's not a lie in my heart.

I focus on telling as much truth as I can.

"I can't marry Iona because I love someone else."

Mama gasps and puts a hand to her throat. Papa's frown deepens on his forehead. "What are you talking about, Ajax? You've never mentioned any girl and you're not dating anyone as we all know. You're home every day and night."

"It's Bridget Walker, isn't it?" Elena leaps out of her chair. "I knew it. You're in love with the American girl."

"The girl from the *Internet*?" Papa asks, his tone sharp. He makes the word "Internet" sound as if it's a brothel.

I shift backward in my seat, a surge of anger shooting through me at how he's diminishing my and Bridget's relationship. Or friendship. Whatever.

My next words come out with a bitter sound. "We met in person in Italy. She's not a girl from the *Internet*. And even if I met her on the Internet, I still love her."

"That's ridiculous," Papa snorts. "You're marrying a nice Greek girl. You can't marry just anyone."

"She's not just anyone," I say trying to stay calm.

Mama puts up her hands. "Ajax, we're watching out for your well-being."

"He's watching out for the farm, you mean." I hate that I sound like a defiant child, but I'm pissed off.

Papa puts both hands firmly down on the table. "Do you want to forfeit your good standing in the family and community? For a girl you hardly know?"

I blink. This is getting way out of hand. For a fake relationship.

But it does make me ask myself some serious questions.

Suppose Bridget and I really were a couple? Suppose we really did want to get married?

Are there obstacles that would rise between us that are harder to overcome than distance?

"Papa and Mama, with all due respect, I love Bridget and I cannot marry Iona. And, I've invited Bridget to visit us for the summer. She wants to help with the farm."

Elena squeals. Mama straightens her back. Papa's face looks like he's Zeus about to lightning bolt me to my chair.

"What kind of help?" he growls.

"With the *Internet*," I say. I would laugh if I could at the expression on Papa's face.

I can see the warrior he once was when he first took over Christos Farms and was determined to make it the best olive oil producer in Greece.

"It's the future of marketing, Papa. She's going to make sure Christos Farms gets on the global map."

"We'll see about that." He stands up. "Any more surprises?"

I shake my head.

"What am I going to tell Mr. Galanis now?" he says softly, almost as if his heart is breaking.

"The truth?" I offer. "Tell him I'm already engaged, but I wish them the best."

A defeated sigh escapes his lips. "Fine. But you'd better know what you're doing, Ajax. Don't tie all our hopes and dreams for a future on a fickle heart."

I cringe inwardly. "I won't."

Mama puts her hands on top of Papa's, showing her solidarity with her husband. "I have something to add."

I swallow hard. I'd thought I was home free to move forward with my and Bridget's fake relationship plans.

"Yes?" I ask quietly.

"One summer," she says, holding up her pointer finger in the air. "To prove this girl Bridget is really the love of your life and that the two of you can save Christos Farms from its spiraling debt."

"Or?" I choke out.

"Or we go back to Plan A."

Elena's almost in tears as she stares at me. She's the one who knows how often Bridget and I speak every day. She may have an inkling of my real feelings for the girl on the other side of the world.

"Exactly," Papa and Mama say together. Like they'd planned it.

"Does that sound fair?" Mama asks as if I have a choice.

I nod. "Sure."

I give them a confident smile. Inside I'm shaking like an olive branch in high wind.

I have one summer for Bridget to save me from an arranged marriage. One summer to see if she can love me for real. One summer to rescue Christos Farm.

"When is she arriving? I need to get her room ready. Order some wonderful bath products for her. Find out her favorite dishes. I hope she likes seafood." Mama asks all this with a smile, switching into Greek hosting mode.

I stagger from the table, muttering I'll get back to her on the dates. I can't make it to my room fast enough to collapse on my bed.

When I'm there I stare up at the ceiling my mind whirling with the possibilities. I remind myself that this thing with Bridget is fake. It's not real.

So even if we succeed in saving Christos Farms, I could still — *will still* — end up with a broken heart.

Plan C begins to take shape in my head.

"Don't fall in love with her buddy," I say aloud in the darkening room. "Do what needs to be done, have one last wonderful summer of your life, and let her go. She does not love you and she never will. Even if she does, the obstacles between you are pretty much insurmountable."

Why must love be so difficult? I groan and close my eyes.

I'm fully dressed and too tired to get up and change. But not too tired to say a prayer.

Somewhere in the middle of my prayer, I catch a glimpse of a star outside my window. It's the first star of the night. The farthest star in the galaxy.

It winks at me in its struggle to be visible. Like it's reminding me there's always a beacon of light in the darkness.

Chapter Fourteen

BRIDGET

After Ajax told me how his announcement went down — like a ton of bricks! — I'm determined not to make the same mistake of blurting out my summer plans any old way.

Timing is everything.

I've already decided to wait until after Daisy's high school graduation to tell my family the news. But now I plan on slipping it into regular conversation so no one can make a big deal about it.

It's a summer vacation in Greece, after all. I'm not going on a space mission.

The actual graduation ceremony is held at the school, and our immediate family is sitting side by side, minus Daisy who is in her cap and gown with her class.

It feels strange being surrounded by all my sisters again. Ava is back from Italy. Corrine is back from college. And, of course, Emerald is in the middle, bringing Ava and Corrine up to speed on her and Jackson's blossoming relationship.

I give myself props for not rolling my eyes or prophesizing

about whether the relationship will survive a summer of Jackson traveling with his family.

When Daisy, looking like a fresh-faced, real-life flower crosses the stage, Ava leans over and whispers in my ear, "You did great, Bridget. This is all you."

I blush. It's good to be recognized for holding down the fort while Ava, the most organized sister, and mother hen to us all, was away.

"Thanks," I whisper.

"I'm glad you and Tyler made it back in time to see Daisy walk the stage. It means a lot to her."

"I wouldn't miss this." Ava shifts to snap a photo and I sit back and congratulate myself. I had my doubts about whether I could support and guide two teenage girls, but hey, we all survived.

After the ceremony, we arrive at the house to find our backyard packed with relatives from Boston and New York. Aunts and uncles from Dad's and Mom's sides are all here, long lines of cousins in their wake.

Dad has hired a caterer so I'm free to mingle and walk around.

I stop to chat with my favorite cousins, Twinkie and JoJo, from Boston who I see regularly when I go down for gallery openings and film festivals.

Twinkie's real name is Tinkerbell, I kid you not. JoJo is short for Joelle. They're sisters and the same ages as me and Ava — 23 and 25.

"I see Ava's back from Italy," Twinkie says dramatically, gesturing with her champagne glass. "With a *hunk*."

I chuckle. "Tyler Donovan. Her boyfriend. He's exceptionally nice."

JoJo shakes her head. "No one who looks like that is nice."

"He is, trust me."

"Well, it's great to see her smiling and in love, after all she's been through." Twinkie takes a sip and realizing what she's brought up, her face flames and she coughs hard. "I'm sorry."

"It's okay," I say. Even though it will *never* be okay.

We all get quiet remembering that day when we were standing in this same spot but for a funeral instead.

I change the subject with the first thing I can think of. "Did you hear I'm going to Greece for the summer?"

Shoot! This was not the ideal way to announce the news. Telling cousins instead of sisters first?

Twinkie and JoJo squeal and barrage me with questions.

"What's all the excitement over here?" Ava asks as she and Corrine stroll over to our group.

"Bridget's going to Greece! Can you believe it? That's like my dream trip." Twinkie can barely contain her excitement. Her eyes are bubbling more than her champagne.

Ava's mouth drops open. Corrine reaches over and closes it for her. It was so swift no one else noticed.

"I was going to tell everyone later," I say. "But I'm planning on going for the summer. Now that both of you are back home."

Ava's eyes are round. "Are you going to see *Ajax*?"

I nod, a smile breaking across my face at the mention of his name.

Geez girl, don't be so obvious.

Corrine raises her perfectly arched eyebrows at me. "Is love brewing in the land of the gods?"

I shake my head fast. "No way. We're friends. I'm going to help him out with the rebranding of his olive oil products. That's all."

Twinkie chortles, "Sure you are. With a name like Ajax, he's bound to be a hunk. Like you know who over there." Her glance shifts over to Tyler who is chatting with our father next to the dessert station.

Ava's face is infused with heat, turning her light brown skin as red as an autumn leaf.

I giggle. Corrine rests a hand on Ava's shoulder, "It's okay to be dating a good-looking dude, sis. It's not a crime."

"Let's stick to Bridget's summer plans, please." Ava slides Corrine's hand off her shoulder.

"What's this I hear about Bridget having summer plans?" Dad strolls up with Tyler next to him. "Please tell me I'm not losing another daughter as soon as one comes back home."

Corrine nods vigorously. "You are Dad." She puts her arms around him. "Deal with it."

"When do you leave?" Ava asks softly. "I was looking forward to having a lot of sister time. I've missed you guys so much."

"Same," Corrine adds.

I glare at Corrine. "You see me every week."

She shrugs. "I still missed you when I was away in the dorms."

My glare deepens. "You can come visit me then. If you missed me that much."

Corrine instantly perks up. "Can I, Dad?" she asks.

I groan. I totally fell into that trap.

"Can she what?" Daisy asks.

She and Emerald arrive at our sides, with Daisy holding a massive piece of cake on a plate and Emerald licking frosting from around the edges. It's good to see them close again after the Jackson drama of the past month.

Maxine, Dad's girlfriend, joins our group, handing Dad a beer and Daisy a large napkin to wipe her frosting-stained cheeks, I presume.

So much for perfect timing. I have to make the announcement now whether I like it or not.

"Okay, folks," I eye the group feeling a bit like Maria in *The Sound of Music* when she's surrounded by the entire von Trapp family and breaks into song about a few of her favorite things.

"Bridget?" Dad's voice pulls me out of my trance.

I clear my throat. "Where was I? Right, I'm going to Greece. To Aegina, a small island. To help my best friend save his olive farm."

Total silence.

From the look of shock on everyone's face, this is not the time to mention I'll also be Ajax's fake fiancée.

"You can't be serious," Emerald says with all the superiority of a new senior in high school. "You can't even plant a flower and you want to go work on a *farm*?"

Dad's nodding his head in agreement, too speechless to add his own view on the topic.

But Maxine smiles kindly. "How wonderful you're going to help your friend," she says.

Daisy turns toward Maxine. "On a *farm!*"

"I think it sounds fun," Twinkie adds.

"I agree," JoJo joins in. "It's Greece, who cares about whether she works on a farm?"

Ava's nodding like she knows a secret. And Tyler is busy texting someone. Probably Ajax, his best friend, to get the inside scoop.

I throw up my arms. "I'm not going to be working on the farm itself. I'm doing the rebranding for their products on social media. That's it. I'll be working on my phone as usual. Not hoisting a pitchfork through the fields."

Emerald sighs. "Thank goodness. I was worried for the olives."

I bat her arm. "Not funny."

Dad reaches through the group and pulls me into one of his famous bear hugs. "My baby. You're going so far. But what an opportunity. I'm so proud of you for putting yourself out there with your work. You're multi-talented, Bridget. Between your amazing voice and your talent for marketing, you have so much to share with the world."

Tears spring to my eyes. I didn't even realize Dad paid attention to what I did. He hardly uses his phone except when he did online dating for a month and met Maxine.

"Thanks, Dad," I hiccup around the lump in my throat.

He pats my back. "You're still going to be my Bridgie Bean, right?"

I groan out loud. "Don't spoil it, Dad. You were doing so well."

His deep laugh rumbles through me. Then, I'm surrounded by all my sisters, their arms reaching across each other to get in on this family hug.

I smile at my good fortune to come from this bunch. They understand how important it is to cherish the moments and celebrate the wins.

Traveling to Greece to save Ajax from an arranged marriage would be a win.

For him. Not for me.

I'm helping a friend in need. Nothing more. Nothing less.

Chapter Fifteen

AJAX

I wake up singing along to every song on the radio.

It's Saturday and Bridget arrives this afternoon. I've managed to get past my fears of our plans falling apart and I'm ready to embrace this experience fully.

If we fail, I want to know I gave it my all before I marry someone I don't know.

It's amazing how fast everything fell into place over the past two weeks once we set our plan in motion.

After I explained that Bridget would try to help us turn around our financials with her great marketing ideas, my parents were more receptive to us getting engaged.

Or as Papa said, "We won't tell Mr. and Mrs. Galanis you're engaged. Americans are fickle. This girl Bridget may not be a small island girl. She may run off as soon as island fever sets in."

I roll my eyes. "We're forty minutes by fast ferry to Athens, Papa. It's hard to get island fever when you can head down to the port and be in one of the world's most significant cultural destinations in less than an hour."

That's what I said logically.

Inside my head, I applauded Papa's bullseye accuracy in describing Bridget.

One thing I knew for sure . . . Bridget is not a small island girl. She's not a farm girl. Bridget is a big-city, center-of-the-excitement kind of girl.

She likes to be around artsy people and her phone.

There are whole areas of this island where broadband or wireless haven't even been introduced yet.

There are villages where only sheep and goats can be found, and the odd person you run into there thinks talking is overrated.

No, we Aegina citizens are friendly and welcoming to tourists. But overall, this island is a haven for peace-seekers.

We aren't Santorini or Mykonos or even Paros, the new "It" spot.

Aegina, despite being so close to Athens, and packed with everything visitors love — beaches, temples, food, and nightlife (sort of), is overlooked for the far-flung islands that require a more strenuous journey to access.

We accept it. We embrace it. We thrive on the peace and quiet.

I'm not so sure Bridget will though.

"I hope she doesn't get bored of *me*," I mumble softly.

"Are you talking to yourself, son?"

Papa peers over the newspaper at me.

We've finished up our early chores and are taking a quick break on the stone patio in the shade of flowering trees before I head inside to review the computer reports while he drives around on his beloved tractor, personally checking on the olives.

The most hi-tech development Papa has incorporated into his drive-bys in twenty years is using his cell to take photos of anything worrisome and sending them to me via text messaging.

It was Elena who taught him that. With patience and determination.

Now, Papa loves sending me photos of trees, lizards, puddles, and even birds.

I shudder for the day he discovers selfies!

"No, Papa, I'm not talking to myself. I was singing."

"Oh!" He shakes out his paper. "Is that what that noise was? You really must be in love."

I ignore him and continue singing along to the radio. Out the side of my eye, I see a small smile quirking on his lips.

A stab of guilt hits me. I'm lying to my family!

I shake my head to dispel that thought.

I'm not lying. I adore Bridget. Since we're pretending to be a couple, I'll show her how being together could really be.

Maybe fate has sent me this opportunity to knock down the walls she has staunchly built around her heart.

She made it clear in Italy that I was only good for a hook-up.

Which didn't happen because I'm probably the only man who'd turn down a hook-up with a beautiful girl on principle.

Another love song blares out on the radio waves. A song about how falling in love is so easy with the right woman.

"Yeah, whatever," I mutter.

"What did you say?" Papa asks.

"Nothing, Papa, nothing."

I'm greeted with a deep frown. Papa glances at the old watch on his wrist. "What time are you going to meet your future wife?"

I cringe inside. I wish Bridget really was my future wife.

"She's not arriving until this afternoon. Are you trying to get rid of me?"

"No." His frown digs deeper into his forehead.

"What is troubling you, Ajax? You're talking to yourself. Muttering, 'whatevers,' and singing like a lovesick donkey."

I scratch my head. Papa doesn't miss a thing. He has the x-ray vision of a multi-generational farmer.

"You want to go for a tractor ride, son? Like the old days?" he chuckles.

If I wasn't so full of excitement mixed with pent-up anxiety about seeing Bridget again, I'd ask him if he was kidding. But I leap up.

"Let's go."

Papa gets nimbly out of his old wooden rocker. "That's right, son. Spend time with your papa outside in the forest instead of burying your face inside that silver apple."

"It's called a laptop."

He scoffs. "I don't like how it smells."

"Laptops don't have a scent."

He nods. "That's what's wrong with them. They smell like nothing."

I roll my eyes at him.

He swings one leg over the tractor seat, and I leap in behind him. "Don't let me be late," I warn as Papa hits the gas pedal, and we rumble off between the trees.

Chapter Sixteen

BRIDGET

I read the autographed book about sailing into your sunset years cover to cover on my long flight to Athens. The author seems to be speaking to me personally.

Although that's what the best books do. Speak to you. I shouldn't be surprised.

I wonder if Mom would have liked it. I spin the book around in my hands, unwilling to let go of its power yet.

I close my eyes and pull forth one of the messages in the chapter on "Owning Your Power."

Everything you need to succeed in your life is already inside you. Your job is to recognize your power, own it, and put it to good use. No one can diminish your personal power except for you. So don't do it!

I wish I knew what my personal power is. How do some people figure out what they're meant to do? What their purpose in life is? And some other folks have no clue? Like me.

Mom owned her power. How many times I heard her say she was a student of life. She took courses online or in-person — to learn something new — gardening, making ice cream, building bookcases, refinishing furniture, and even mechanics to fix her and Dad's cars herself.

She'd have her books propped up next to her, pages dirty with her smudges.

I stare out the tiny airplane window at dark space.

I never wanted to plant flowers or build a bookcase or fix a flat with Mom. Although she offered to teach me.

I didn't think it was important. That practical stuff was secondary compared to learning song lyrics to the musicals I aspired to be in.

Neither of us imagined that one day I'd be off to Greece to spend a summer on an olive farm.

I think Mom would have prepared me for this adventure. She'd have . . . I don't know . . . taught me the difference between a trowel and a spade?

For my part, I'd have paid attention to Mom. I'd have mastered a few basic things. I'd have borrowed some of Mom's power. If I could do it all over again, I would have tried to learn stuff from her.

If.

I glance at the sailboat on the book cover. It looks exactly like the yacht I saw in my daydream — the one in which Ajax and his mysterious wife were embarking on their life together.

I whisper, "What do you want from me?"

The book stays silent.

Except for six words rolling through my mind:

Your greatest power is knowing yourself.

As the plane heads toward a red dawn, I make a silent promise to myself to try and figure it out.

Chapter Seventeen

AJAX

When Bridget steps off the ferry, all rational thought escapes my brain. I want to race over and grab her, hold her close and never let her go. Never let her leave me or Aegina.

A whooshing noise like highway traffic fills my ears as if Fate herself has landed on my shoulder and is hissing into my ear. I must make Bridget mine.

I wish I knew how to do that.

I dodge disembarking passengers with their rollie bags and boxes to get closer to her.

She looks up and catches sight of me waving. I'm taller than most so she can't miss me. Plus, I'm swinging a large olive branch above my head like a goofball. We'd agreed on this signal. She was scared she wouldn't locate me in the crowd.

The biggest smile comes over her brown face. Her eyes, even from this distance, are starry bright.

Oh, my heart. My poor busted-up heart. It doesn't stand a chance if — *when* — she leaves me.

An unexpected sadness rips through my body at the thought of having to say goodbye to her again right here in three months. I stuff it down so I can greet her properly after her long journey to reach me.

"I can't believe you're here!" I exclaim as I lift Bridget's slim body in my arms and spin her around. It's a good thing we're fake dating. There's no way I wasn't going to snatch her up and hold her close.

"I'm here!" she sings back. "Seriously, dude, this place is incredible. I can't believe how blue your water is. And this sky." Bridget points upward. "I've never seen anything so clean and clear and . . . blue!"

She won't look directly into my eyes. I wonder if our reunion is as emotional for her as it is for me. Whether she feels even a tiny bit of the joy and sadness I'm feeling simultaneously. Is she asking the Universe, like I am, why my perfect person has to live so far away?

I force myself to stop with all the internal musings and give her my biggest grin.

I lower her back onto the concrete wharf. I'm reluctant to let her go, but I can't keep gripping her so tightly like a possessed man.

My throat constricts.

She's so gorgeous. Like a mermaid with her disheveled curls and sea-green leggings.

But she's much more than a pretty package.

During the ups and downs of the past six months, speaking to Bridget every day balanced out the stress.

The joyful way in which she talked about her sisters and her hometown, her father, and his new girlfriend. Even her good-hearted grumbling about some dude named Jackson. Her spirit gave me a welcome break from my struggles.

And now here she is in person. I want to tell her how much it means to be standing here holding her hands instead of holding a phone.

I can't do that.

I'd sound like a clingy idiot. Chase her away.

I'm not saying or doing anything to mess this up.

"You're choking me I can't breathe." Bridget pulls back and smacks my upper arm. Oh shoot, I didn't realize I'd grabbed her close again.

"Wimp," I tell her, my face covered in smiles. I can't help it. I'm grinning like I woke up and all my wishes have come true.

"Let's get your bags and get out of here."

"Woo hoo! Ajax is that you? Can you help me with my bag?"

I glance over at an older woman dragging a carry-on. "Hold on, Bridge, that's Mrs. Kouris, my teacher from high school. I'll be right back."

I end up helping Mrs. Kouris and two of her cousins lug their bags to the sidewalk where they can catch a taxi.

I race back to Bridget who is taking photos of the ferry chugging its way out of port. Passengers wave goodbye to Aegina from the top level.

"How was your trip?" I ask as I steer her rolling suitcase down the concrete wharf.

She ambles along next to me and I slow down to match her pace.

Her head swivels left to right taking in the sights.

"Wow, Ajax, you didn't tell me it was so picture postcard looking. Or should I say, so 'Instagrammable.'"

I grin. "I wanted to manage your expectations."

"Consider them managed."

June in Aegina brings in a fresh sea breeze, but also a wave of Athenians starting their summer holidays in their second homes.

The waterfront is crowded, filled with cruise ship passengers who've come over from the Piraeus port in Athens for a day trip to the island.

"It's so busy," she says cheerfully. "I wasn't expecting this many people."

I don't tell her that's only in Aegina town. She'll see soon enough.

We walk past fishing boats showcasing their fresh catch of the day.

"Is that . . . ?" Bridget peers closer at the fishing lines strung up between boats. The fishermen and their wives have hung up fresh octopi with clothes pins to dry in the sun. The tentacles wave about in the breeze.

She gulps.

"You don't like octopus?"

"Never had it."

I'm not surprised. None of my friends at Harvard had ever tasted octopus either.

"They're a standard food here. Grilled, stewed, fried. It's delicious."

She puts a hand on her chest. "I always thought an octopus was a gigantic thing with long tentacles."

I chuckle. "That's in Disney movies."

She looks around and shrugs, "Well, this place looks like a Disney set. Tell me I'm wrong. And you look like a Disney prince."

She smacks a hand over her mouth. "Sorry, I don't mean to objectify you."

I grin. I don't tell her I was thinking the same thing about her. That she looks like a Disney princess, but better because she's real.

"The Jeep's this way." We cross the road carefully in between scooters, horses, and taxis.

When we get to the other side, Bridget stops in her tracks. "No way!"

"What?" We're standing in front of one of Aegina's many souvenir shops that feature the island's products.

Huge cellophane bags of pistachios are piled high on top of each other on a wooden table outside the shop.

She points. "Are those pistachios? My absolute favorite snack in the world?"

"Your favorite snack? How did I not know that about you?"

She nods, her eyes alight with a look I know too well. Elena gets it when she wants to eat more than she can possibly handle.

"Well, come on then." I walk her over to the shop run by my Uncle Theo, who is Papa's younger brother. "I might know the owner," I grin.

Uncle Theo is busy talking to a couple. Bridget looks around, eyes wide at Aegina's many products for sale. Her eyes land on Christos' Olive Oil set out in our brand-new bottles.

"This is yours?" Her eyes are shining, like she found gold.

I nod. A smile lurks at the corners of my mouth. I'm ridiculously proud of our homegrown, homemade, organic product.

She picks one up. "Take a picture of me!"

I laugh. "Now? There's more where that came from. I kinda know the guy . . ."

"Hush, Ajax. Photo. Now! Where's your phone!"

I snap a couple of pics and send them to her phone. I set one of the photos — Bridget with a big smile on her face, curls wild, a bottle of olive oil held high like she's presenting it as a trophy, so awkward but so damn adorable — as my new screensaver.

Uncle Theo wraps up his sale and the couple leaves with heavy bags.

He turns to us as I'm slipping my phone into my back pocket.

"Ju ju, did you bring me something new for the shop?" He pats my shoulders which are at least two feet higher than his. I swear I was adopted.

"Ju ju?" Bridget swings around and mouths my old nickname to me, a cheeky look in her eyes.

"No!" I say loudly. "We said we'd come up with *new* nicknames. Ju ju is off-limits."

Uncle Theo turns around fully. "Ju ju is never off limits. Now, tell me, who is this ravishing Greek goddess you've got with you?"

Bridget steps forward, her arm outstretched. "Hi, I'm Bridget Walker, Ajax's . . . ." she stops.

"My fiancée," I add.

Bridget's face flushes.

The shock on Uncle Theo's face is comical. His eyes bulge out. His moustache quivers.

He reaches for a cell phone sitting on the counter and presses a button. In seconds, he's jabbering in Greek so loudly that I feel sorry for whoever's on the other end.

Although I have a good idea who it is.

Almost before Uncle Theo can close off the call, my aunt appears. "Ju ju. You're getting married!"

Aunt Zoe wraps thick arms around me and squeezes me hard.

"Finally, a wedding in the family! I hope it'll rub off on your cousins. Is this her?"

She has barely stopped hugging me before Aunt Zoe scoops up Bridget and squeezes her too.

"This is Bridget. My . . . fiancée." My tongue gets caught on the roof of my throat.

Bridget side-eyes me.

Aunt Zoe looks me up and down. "And when is the engagement party? I didn't hear a thing about this. What are your Papa and Mama thinking keeping this a secret? I'm calling them right now."

She goes to pick up the phone but I beg, something you have to do a lot of in my family if you want to control your own fate.

"Please Aunt Zoe, Bridget arrived a few minutes ago. We will call everyone after we get settled. I promise. We need to make plans. But you won't be left out."

"We need a save-the-date thingie, like what they do in America."

Aunt Zoe watches a lot of American television. She thinks *Friends* is a reality show.

Bridget hugs my aunt with one arm. "That's a great idea. Ajax and I will work on our save-the-date cards tonight."

I mouth silently over Aunt Zoe's head, "We will not!"

Bridget ignores me.

"We'll invite everyone! Send me the list of family members. Can you do that for us? We really need your help." Bridget says this like she's planned engagement parties before.

I raise an eyebrow at her.

"Right, my dear?" she purrs, patting my chest with her long tapered turquoise nails.

"Of course, my love, anything you want."

Aunt Zoe beams at us. I feel awful there isn't going to be an engagement party.

Bridget laughs a tinkly, happy laugh. I can't tell if it's real or fake. It has to be fake, right?

And what does she mean we're inviting everyone? Does she have any idea how many aunts and uncles and cousins that would include?

My family would put *The Big Fat Greek Wedding* movie to shame.

We say our goodbyes and I hustle Bridget out of Uncle Theo's shop as quickly as possible before more family members show up.

We're halfway to my Jeep when Bridget stops in mid-stride, her brown face paling considerably and she wails, "I didn't buy my pistachios!"

My heart skips a beat. I swore she was going to say something awful. Like she wants to go back home.

I drop the suitcase and race back to the shop in two seconds flat. I grab the first bag of pistachios I can put a hand on and yell to Uncle Theo, "I'll pay you later," before dashing back to Bridget.

I hold up the clear bag of sleek nuts as a prize. "Got them."

She blinks. "Are you always this accommodating? Dude, a woman could get used to your knightly behavior."

"You mean my good manners?"

"Yes, well that, too."

I grin. "It's just for your first day. Tomorrow I go back to being an ogre."

She wrinkles her nose at me as she searches for a seatbelt in the man cave that is my personal vehicle.

"Sorry, hold on. I reach up and grab the seat belt and slash it across her body, clipping it in soundly. My face is so close to hers that when I look up under my lashes, her lips are mere centimeters away. Her eyes stare into mine as if caught in headlights.

An entire minute passes in which we just breathe.

I would give anything to tilt my head and kiss her soft lips.

Her lips tremble as I stare at them. Like they want me to kiss them.

A soft groan escapes her mouth. "I wish . . ."

"What?" I whisper, needing to cough but not daring to in case I break the spell.

"I wish . . . you'd get a move on. I'm exhausted."

I blink. That was not what she was about to say before. I may not know everything about Bridget, but I do recognize when she's not being upfront.

After months of talking every day on the phone, where all you can do is listen and watch every facial expression, you learn when your best friend is hiding something.

What could she be hiding? Secret feelings for me maybe? Or for someone else?

I peel myself away before my thoughts get any weirder.

"Strange, isn't it?" I say, in my best fake jovial manner. "Being able to sit next to each other instead of staring at a phone screen."

She nods but doesn't say anything else. I wrestle with the steering wheel, downshifting as we turn to drive up the coastal road. Have I offended her somehow?

We're going to need some rules, so I don't mess up my part of this "fake" relationship.

In my heart, where it counts, it's all real to me.

Chapter Eighteen

BRIDGET

Whoa! That was a close call. I truly must be tired to have come so close to kissing my best friend.

I'm sure it was a combination of the long flight, the difference in time zones, and the fact that I'm trying to balance being a bestie with being a fake fiancée.

There's no other reason I would act so thirsty, yearning for Ajax's sexy lips.

Not to mention I almost moaned his name out loud. Like what the hell!

Jet lag is what I'm feeling. Nothing more.

I stare out the passenger window of Ajax's Jeep Wrangler, struggling to reorganize my emotions.

The Jeep is blue, with huge tires and mud streaks all around the doors as if it's constantly being driven through the dirt. Which it probably is.

In Italy, Ajax was a cool city dude, in a black leather jacket and jeans.

Here, he's sporting shorts, a t-shirt fitted across his broad chest, and a bandana tied around his neck. Like that guy John B. in *Outer Banks*, my and Ava's favorite Netflix show.

Ajax is a taller, beefier version of John B. but they have the same unruly curls and devil-may-care clothing style.

If I didn't know Ajax, I'd be stalking him. Internet stalking . . . not real-life stalking, although I wouldn't take that off the table either.

I've been trying to play it cool since I stepped off the ferry and he picked me up and spun me around like we were a real couple starring in our own Netflix romance.

But it's definitely harder than I thought it would be — playing it safe with him. Especially when the bronzed hair on his muscular forearm tickles my arm.

Tingles race through my body, at his mere touch. Something that's never happened to me before.

I could move my arm away. I could and I should!

I can't go breaking this guy's heart. No matter how handsome and woke and kind he is.

I'm here on a mission. To help him and his family save their olive farm. And to stop his arranged marriage.

That's it.

Getting a chance to enjoy a beautiful Greek island is a perk.

Kissing Ajax is NOT!

Chapter Nineteen

AJAX

I have no idea what she's thinking. None!

She's staring out the passenger window like a lamb off to the slaughter.

I want to squeeze her hand and reassure her that it'll be fine.

Except, I'm confused.

We didn't plan out how our fake relationship would work. We were too busy organizing the logistics of her trip while I worked on breaking the news to my family and dealing with the aftermath.

Now, here we are, and in twenty minutes we'll be home, and we still haven't discussed our status.

All of this is making me drive a little faster around the curves and up and down the hills than I normally would.

When she grabs hold of the strap at the top of her window, I release my foot from the gas pedal and gear down.

"Sorry," I say.

She gives me a tight smile. "It's okay. I'm watching the scenery."

I gaze out the windows imagining I'm seeing my island for the first time through her eyes.

Does she notice all the tiny chapels alongside the gravelly roadways?

Or the kids leaping off the boulders into the shimmering blue sea?

Or the rock terraces, looking like giant steps to the sky?

Does she smell the evergreen pines as we get closer to my farm?

When we pass a field of pistachio trees, I point them out to her.

"Aegina has the world's best pistachios."

"I bet you say that to all the girls," she giggles, breaking her silence.

I laugh with relief. "We do. Google it."

She holds up her bag and stares at it the way I wish she'd look at me. Am I seriously jealous of a bag of nuts?

"I'd never even heard of Aegina before I met you."

"I know. It's one of the best-kept secrets of Greece."

"So are you," she says.

I'm just about to hoot with laughter when out of nowhere she leans over straining against her seat belt and kisses my cheek.

I wish she'd warned me. I swing the steering wheel hard to avoid knocking over one of the blue and white mini chapels on the side of the road.

Her bag of pistachios flies out of her hands and hits the floor.

"Dude!"

"Sorry. Next time, warn a fella."

"Got it. I'll announce it first. Incoming kiss, prepare."

I grin at her. "Better."

"But seriously," I wave my arm out the window at the endless fields of pistachio trees. I slow down to a crawl. There are no other cars around anyway.

"Pistachios are an important part of our local economy. I've been considering planting some pistachio trees to supplement our income. Diversify our crops."

Bridget turns her body to me. "That's a great idea. I would so move here to eat pistachios every day!"

I raise an eyebrow at her. "Done!"

"We can tell everyone, 'You had me at pistachios.'"

We laugh together, the ice completely broken, the heavy scent of pine needles filling our heads.

The low-level anxiety I'd been feeling has disappeared. I reach for her hand and she slips her warm one into mine.

"I think we should practice for when we get to my house."

"What's to practice? We know almost everything about each other," she says and settles back into her seat.

Suddenly I want our drive to last a lot longer.

We're heading toward the mountain of Zeus. A detour will take us to my second favorite place in the world, the Temple of Aphaia.

I'd planned to show it to Bridget with a picnic and wine to watch the sunset, but now, I can't wait for her to see it.

The entire West Pediment of the temple had sculptures and carvings dedicated to the War of Troy featuring the warrior Ajax, my namesake.

"I have something to show you," I tell her.

She drops her head onto my shoulder. She covers a large yawn with the back of a hand. "I'm sorry. Can we see it tomorrow? I want to be properly awake when I see the sights of Aegina."

My heart clenches. Of course, she's exhausted. What am I thinking?

I make a U-turn in the middle of the deserted road before the temple.

It's as glorious as Poseidon and Athena's ancient temples in Athens.

"Next time," I say, as I hear her breathing slowing down.

Her presence is like a warm blanket I didn't know I was missing.

The Temple and beaches and olives and all the island's treasures will have to wait.

I want her to fall in love with Aegina for real. Even if she won't be falling in love with me.

Chapter Twenty

BRIDGET

I must have dozed off because the last thing I remember is talking about pistachios.

I have no idea how we ended up in front of these massive stone walls, with a remote-controlled gate. The gate is decorated with elaborate trees made of wrought iron. It looks like something out of a fairy tale.

With a flick of Ajax's wrist, the gate slides apart for us to drive through.

The scene before me takes my breath away.

I don't know where to look first. On my left is a large pond with ducks and geese and a statue in the middle spouting water.

To my right is a vast green lawn. We drive along the road (I can't call it a driveway) for a couple of minutes, passing what must be the olive groves on either side of the roadway.

As far as I can see are rows of green trees, exactly like the ones I saw on my phone when Ajax and I spoke, but I had no idea there'd be so many!

It's a serious forest.

Further up ahead is a large stone structure. It must be his home, but it looks like a mansion. The house sprouts stone wings in every direction. Balconies, patios, and terraces connect earth and sky.

"Who are you, people?" I gasp.

Ajax slides the gear shift into park. I open my door and hop out.

Ajax steps out next to me. "Welcome to Christos Farms," he says solemnly like we're in a church.

"Sorry, I'm confused. You're rich!" I say it almost accusingly. Like why did he need me? He's loaded.

Ajax shakes his head. "The home was built over four generations — you'll see for yourself how crazy it is, nothing matches in there — but it's the land that's worth money and it's the land I want to keep farming.

"I don't want to sell off any of it to pay bills. Plus, I need to keep the farm running with the new technology to help eliminate CO2 from the atmosphere. Our farm has almost a zero-carbon footprint." His last words are said with great pride.

I walk around in a circle. We're still far away from the house.

"Christos Farms looks amazing," I say honestly. "I had no idea it was so immense. No wonder you were always out in the fields working hard."

He leans a forearm against the top of the Jeep. His bicep bulges out, but I try to ignore the muscles. I'm not here to gawk.

"I was constantly teasing you about being sweaty." I cover my face with my hands.

His dark eyes twinkle.

"I was so foolish. You have a legacy you're saving and doing it with no damage to the environment. In fact, you're helping the environment."

He nods.

"And I was telling you to put on a shirt."

He grins. "Bridget, I loved when you teased me. You make me laugh. You made this past year bearable."

I feel close to tears for some strange reason. But I don't do tears. I'm logical. The clear-headed, unemotional sister. I'm here to help promote a business. Not to get attached to this man.

Time to pivot to the business angle.

"Right. I'm glad I'm seeing this in person. I'll need all my skills to do justice to your olive oil business."

He reaches out his big arms and hugs me. "I'm just glad you're here."

I snuggle in close. For no other reason than that, I'm tired. And he feels so good to rest my head on.

Call it business research. Ajax's bright ideas and beautiful smile will feature prominently in the rebranding. Not to mention, maybe a few shirtless pics of him digging around the trees. Or whatever they do here.

Chapter Twenty-One

AJAX

She peppers me with questions as we drive closer to the house. Questions I would never have guessed would be on her mind.

But that goes to show how different we all are, how different we are perceived in the world, and how different we perceive it back.

She asks me, "Do they know I'm American? Did you tell them I am Black?"

I stutter. "What?"

She raises up one of her lovely, toned arms. "My skin color, did you tell them?"

I can feel whatever color I have in my face draining out. "Um . . . no . . . should I have?"

She makes a face at me. "It's very important."

"Oh." I blink and slow down the Jeep. "I can text them before we get there."

A weird laugh escapes her lips. "We have five more minutes

before we reach your home. Is that enough time to prepare them, that their fake future daughter-in-law is not white?"

In the awkward silence filling the vehicle, I turn to her and apologize. Except I'm not sure what I'm apologizing for.

"I didn't think it mattered, Bridge."

Wrong!

The look she throws at me is diabolical. "It matters," she says through gritted teeth.

I swallow around the lump growing in my throat. "I'm truly sorry. How can I fix it? How can I make you feel more comfortable?"

I think back to my years at Harvard with my best friend Tyler Donovan, who is now Bridget's sister's boyfriend.

Tyler is Black. Tyler belonged to the Black Student Association and participated in many cultural activities and marches. He was very vocal about our college's anti-racism policies.

But for me, I was a foreign student on the outskirts of America's issues. It didn't affect me. I have always been an ally to Tyler and the BLM movement because it was the right thing to do, but I wasn't involved like Tyler was.

I watch Bridget fidget with her clothes, fix her lipstick in the mirror and, I don't know . . . prepare herself. But for what?

Possible rejection? As if meeting my family could hurt her and she's got to be ready.

A huge sinking feeling invades me to my core.

I feel ashamed I didn't ask her before now. What I could do?

It never once occurred to me that I should tell my family her race or skin color. To make it a smooth transition for Bridget.

I look over at the gorgeous woman sitting next to me, who is usually laughing and teasing, but now looks worried and nervous.

I straighten my shoulders. I grab her hands and hold them in mine.

"You know what Bridge, we got this. You and me. We're in this together. Fake or real or whatever you want to call our relationship."

I point to her and me. "We're a team. And if anybody gives you grief, anybody makes you feel uncomfortable at all, I want to know."

She shakes her head. "Oh sweetie, I appreciate you. You're awesome. But you can't protect me from other people's ideas of me. Their fears or irrational notions. You can't."

I swallow hard again. "Watch me," I hear the growl in my voice.

She stares at me with her large eyes. "What are you? Jason and the Argonauts, off on a quest for the Golden Fleece, which in this case would be to eradicate racism?"

I turn back and face forward, gripping the steering wheel with tight hands.

"Yes," I say forcefully.

Silent beats pass as she stares at me.

I breathe deeply. "I don't believe it will be an issue at all," I say, trying to calm myself down. Trying to ease her concerns. "Not for my family. Or on Aegina."

In my head though, I'm throwing down the gauntlet to everyone.

I will do whatever it takes to make sure Bridget is welcomed. Not just welcomed. But appreciated for her talents and gifts, her humor, and plain old lovability.

If I must singlehandedly fight to make this world better, I will. For her.

At the same time, I'm thinking how it's a shame these atrocities have to affect someone we love before people like me, whom it doesn't "affect," choose to stand up and fight.

I don't want to be just an ally. I want to be her warrior.

Chapter Twenty-Two

BRIDGET

Holy smokes! I think I'm in love. Never has a man defended me like this.

We're standing in the wide, high-ceiling living room of his family's home and Ajax has his fists curled at his sides.

His eyes are intense beams of light surveying every expression on his parents and sister's faces.

Meanwhile, my shoulders have relaxed, my legs have stopped shaking and my smile is ready and real.

This must be how it feels to have a Greek god, or demi-god, by your side.

But Ajax was right. I needn't have worried. His mother reaches out her arms and hugs me close like I'm family. Her smiles and welcome are genuine. I forget I'm in a fake relationship with her son and smile broadly.

"Thank you for welcoming me to your home," I say. I side-eye Ajax, telepathically telling him to relax.

He doesn't.

He turns to his father and sweeps me forward to meet the patriarch, one arm clasped protectively around my shoulders.

I smile at his dad who has a fierce nose, bushy eyebrows, and the sun-leathered skin of a man who works outdoors and is happy about it.

"Hello, Bridget," he says with his heavy Greek accent. I wonder how my American accent sounds to them.

I feel Ajax's arm tightening around my shoulders. I swear this man is as strong as his chiseled muscles look.

"Hello, Mr. Christos," I greet Ajax's father.

His father looks me right in the eye and declares, "You don't look like a farmer's wife."

The way he grins, his dark eyes alighting with mischief, I can see the younger man he once was.

A terrible jokester and tease. Not that different from Ajax — on a good day when Ajax isn't in super protective mode and squeezing the daylights out of me.

Before I can say another word, Mr. Christos hands me and Ajax a glass of dark liquid from a pretty bottle on the side table.

"Yamas!" he shouts. "Welcome to the family, Bridget Walker."

Mrs. Christos picks up her own tiny glass and raises it high. Ajax looks at me and we raise our eyebrows at each other.

I remember my promise to Daisy before I left home to be open to trying new customs.

"Yamas!" I join in, tipping the glass toward my mouth and swallowing the sweet licorice liquid. I gasp out loud.

"Oh my." My eyes stream water as the liquor sets fire to my throat like a liquid match.

I remember the first time I drank alcohol at a school dance. I was sixteen and I sputtered it out like a fountain. I pray I don't do that again. Although my brain is begging me to do it.

"More ouzo?" Mrs. Christos laughs and reaches for my glass to pour another round.

I hold up two hands in surrender. "Not right now, but thank

you." I struggle to find a way to not seem ungrateful. "Maybe later?" I suggest.

"What about me?" A thin voice trails its way into the cavernous room.

A pixie of a child, half girl, half fairy creature appears in a diaphanous dress holding a sign decorated with glitter and hearts.

I squint to make out the words. "Congratulations Ajax and Bridget!"

"I'm Elena," she announces. Then before I can say hello, she rushes over and presents the sign to me. "I'm so glad I'll be getting a sister."

I put a hand to my throat. A river of guilt floods me. I can't lie to this gorgeous woodland creature.

I glance up at Ajax. He's looking away as if he too can't bear it.

I clear my throat.

"I have four sisters, but I'll gladly add you to the bunch," I tell Elena. Which is true. I would gladly consider Elena a sister.

Her small, pointed face lights up.

She puts a hand in mine and begins leading me out of the living room.

"Okay everyone, it's dinner time and I'm hungry. Bridget is going to sit next to me and tell me about American boys."

A choking sound escapes Ajax's throat.

I grin. "Um . . . well, I don't know too many boys."

"Rubbish," Elena says, as we enter a large room made from ancient wood, probably olive trees, with wooden beam ceilings and what appears to be handmade furniture, gleaming under the overhead lights.

The house, like Elena, is giving off a fairy tale 'lost in the woods' vibe.

I almost feel as if I've entered another world since passing through the elaborate gate.

Dinner is a feast of sights and tastes blindsiding my tiredness.

Baskets of fresh-baked pita are passed around. Surprisingly, the pita is not flat like in Greek restaurants back home. These pitas are small, round puffed pockets of deliciousness.

The salad is massive, with bricks of feta cheese and chunks of ruby red tomatoes the size of my hand. I'm surprised to learn there's no lettuce in real Greek salads.

But there's liters of delicious olive oil fresh from the farm and I'd be satisfied just to soak it up with my pita.

Sizzling meats appear from a grill along with bowls of fava beans and hummus, roasted potatoes, and french fries — crisp and perfect.

I close my eyes and sigh.

"This is the best dinner I think I've ever eaten."

Mrs. Christos beams.

Elena chuckles. "Try the olives." She pushes a bowl of dark objects toward me that I thought were pickles.

My eyes widen. "I scoop up two of the largest olives I've ever seen with a spoon and plop them on my plate. "I almost need a knife and fork for these."

"They're kalamata olives," Ajax informs me. "Not from our farm, but Elena adores them."

I try one. It's robust and delicious.

Throughout the meal, Mr. Christos served us glasses of wine from a decanter on the table. I learn that the wine is from Aegina, made on a neighboring farm from local grapes.

"Everything on the table is grown and made here or from someone's farm in Aegina," Ajax says.

"Except my olives," Elena corrects him.

"Right."

The meal ends with pistachio ice cream made by Elena and Mrs. Christos.

I eat two scoops despite groaning that I couldn't eat another bite, minutes before I tasted the ice cream.

After the dishes are cleared away, with me offering to help and Mrs. Christos saying no in like three different languages, we head over to the living room.

When Mrs. Christos joins us, I tell the family I have something to say.

Everyone gets incredibly quiet. Ajax throws me a worrying glance. He mouths, "What is it?"

I can see from his furrowed brow that he thinks I'm going to spill the beans and declare we're just friends and not real fiancés. Trust me, I have thought of saying exactly that to this loving family.

I wave away his concern like I'm waving from on top of a parade float.

When they're all seated, I stand before them, hands clasped thinking, "Do I really need to say this? Should I leave well enough alone?"

But then I answer myself in my head. "You're here to live with this family for three months."

"Okay, I want to officially say thank you for inviting me to share your amazing home for the summer. Maybe I am not what you expected. I know Ajax did not tell you I am a person of color. But I hope we can talk openly about any concerns you may have. Communication is key."

I'm greeted by three, no make that *four*, frowning faces.

"Bridget," Mrs. Christos says, standing up and holding out her hands. "Your color is glorious. Like a dusky sky or a deep ocean dive. You are the setting sun and the early morning tide. Imagine how much love it took to make a girl as special as you."

I hiccup my budding tears away. "Thank you, Mrs. Christos."

I turn toward the patriarch. Does he feel the same way?

Mr. Christos gets up and pours out two tiny glasses of the ouzo wine. He hands one to me and one to Ajax.

"He's from the 'show, don't tell' school," Elena remarks.

Everyone laughs, including me.

"Drink up Bridget and Ajax. We are happy to support such a fine couple as the two of you." He turns towards his wife and daughter. "I speak for the family. Yamas!"

I look at Ajax and he grins at me. "Drink up sweetie."

I gulp down the tiny glass of searing liquid. It sets fire to my throat as before. I guess this is one drink that'll never get easier to swallow.

And it serves me right to ask Mr. Christos if he's prejudiced. Ha!

I'm ready to drop down with exhaustion after the heavy meal, two glasses of wine, and another shot of ouzo.

Ajax and I sit together on the sofa as his parents share stories about Ajax growing up. I must say I'm shocked at how quickly I've started to think of him as my partner/fiancé.

You've never even kissed the dude, I remind myself.

But he feels so comfortable. Like I've known him forever. My eyes are closing as Ajax's father talks about family and the farm.

I'm fighting to stay awake when I hear a word — two words — that make my eyes pop wide open.

"Engagement party!"

"Bridget!" Mr. Christos is all smiles. "Mrs. Christos and I would like to throw a little engagement *party* for you and Ajax. We'll invite everyone! The family and neighbors, and even Ajax's bowling team."

So much new information is hitting my tired brain I can't decide what to process first.

"You bowl?" I turn on Ajax. "How come you never told me that?"

At the same time, Ajax says, "An engagement party?"

I register his surprise. "A party? For you and me?" I point to his chest then mine. Like I must make sure *we're* the ones engaged.

With his mischievous grin, Mr. Christos rubs his hands together. "Yes, we'll roast a goat and order the best catch from the fishermen. We must celebrate our only son finding the woman he will marry. This is a prominent occasion."

Neither Ajax nor I say another word.

I don't know about Ajax, but I can't let this wonderful family throw what would be a costly island-wide party to celebrate something that isn't real.

But what will happen when Ajax and I come clean?

I look around the room, taking in Mr. and Mrs. Christos's excited faces. Elena's glowing eyes.

We did not think this through.

I'd be banned! I'd never be able to return to this beautiful island again.

As for Ajax, he'd be forced to marry, and he won't have time to be friends with me anymore.

"Why are you not happy? Is a great thing, a party!" Mr. Christos says.

I force a smile on my lips. "It sounds amazing."

"Yes," Ajax chokes out. "Amazing, indeed."

Chapter Twenty-Three

AJAX

"**O**kay, let's stay calm," I tell Bridget, rubbing circles on her back as she leans forward on the sofa in my room, her hands clasped tightly like she's trying to hold herself together.

We've dropped off her bags in the guest suite and I've shown her the basic layout of the sprawling house so she can find her way to my studio and the main living areas.

"I'll need a map," she joked as we went up steps and around corners and down long cool hallways decorated with art from local painters.

"Come find me when you're ready," I told her, leaving reluctantly.

She sits with me now, showered, and changed into pajamas I recognize from our late-night calls. Fluffy pink socks are on her feet, which she's tucked under her.

"How can we stay calm when your parents are planning an engagement party? No, a *feast* for us?"

My hand stops circling and drops into my lap. I take a deep breath. "What are our options?"

She side-eyes me. "We could tell them the truth."

I groan. "It's too late for that. They'd disown me. At least my father would. He would never understand."

She shakes her head. "I guess he doesn't watch any rom-coms."

I bark a laugh. "No, not a one."

We sit in silence. I'm staring at the skylight above my head looking out for that distant star I count on for its unfailing light.

Bridget leans back and settles next to me, tilting her head backward to see what I see.

She turns to me with a smile breaking across her worried features. "You got an amazing setup here, dude. I could get used to this."

She says it like it's nothing. Although her words pierce my soul. I want you to get used to this, I think. But I say nothing. We stare together at the dark night sky above.

"It looks even better from the outside if you want to go check it out."

I point in the direction of the sliding glass door to my personal wooden deck where I've planted rows of flowering plants and strung up a hammock on two wooden beams.

She nods and snuggles next to me. Very much in real fiancée style.

I hold my breath. Does she have a clue what she does to me being so close? I want to scoop her up, plunk her down on my lap and kiss her red lips. Or just hug her close all night sitting here, not moving while she sleeps.

I'm not ready to give up on this yet.

I brush her hair out of her face. "Bridge, do you trust me?"

She looks me in the eye. "Why?"

"I'm asking. Do you trust me?"

She nods slowly.

"Well then let's keep with the plan for the rest of the week and see how it goes. As a farmer, I can tell you, that nature has a way of taking its own course, no matter what you plan. We can anticipate outcomes and mitigate any damages to the crop, but ultimately, it's up to nature."

She looks deep in thought like she's considering what I said.

It's true, too. Nature has a way of working itself out, one way or another. Sometimes — most times — you must allow the greater powers to show you the way.

"Okay," she says, a tiny frown marring her beautiful face. "As long as we pay for our own fake engagement party."

My turn to frown. "I doubt my family will go for that. Especially my mother."

"Tell them I insist. That we saved up for it or something. Anything. If we're saving you from an arranged marriage, paying for a party will be worth it."

"Oh, I'm not worried about whether it's worth it. I'm concerned my parents will refuse."

She leans over and plucks my chin with her slender fingers. "Well, my Greek hero, find a way. Because I draw the line at this."

I nod. Another reason I love this woman. Her integrity is 100 percent.

"Got it. I agree for the record, so I'll insist that they let us pay for the party. This means we'll also move the date. I need more time to organize. And to cut costs I'll go around to all my cousins and pull favors."

Bridget giggled. "You're the godfather of Aegina."

I nod and smile. "Something like that. I can at least get the goat and the fish and most of the other food for free."

"I will handle the decorations."

She muses for a moment then snaps her fingers. "Do you guys have a theater on the island? This is a *Greek* island, so you must."

I nod slowly, not sure where she's going with that idea.

"Cool. Can you take me? And Elena? I'd like to see a bit of

Greek theater while I'm here. More importantly, I can recruit some theater geeks to help with our party decorations."

I grin. "They're not called theater geeks in Greece. They're thespians."

She fake swipes sweat off her brow. "Thespians it is."

The goofy smile leaves her lips replaced by her biting on them.

"What?" I ask, scooping her even closer. "What is it? I know that *'I've got something on my mind look'* of yours."

She nods slowly. "I was just wondering . . ."

"About?"

"Thespians."

"Hmmmm . . . and?"

She shuts her eyes. "Nothing. Just what it must be like to be an honest-to-goodness actress in Greece where theater was invented."

Before I can answer her, I hear soft sleeping sounds escaping her lips. Bridget Walker has fallen asleep in my arms.

I sit back and sigh. This is my dream come true. I'm not going to miss a second of it.

Chapter Twenty-Four

BRIDGET

The next day, I wake up in the luxurious guest suite with no idea how I got here. The last thing I remember is talking to Ajax and feeling his protective arms around me.

As I pull on shorts, a t-shirt, and sneakers, I remember our mission to throw our own engagement party. But another thought tickles the back of my brain.

Something to do with the theater. With *Greek* theater. Is it possible I might see an actual Greek play this summer?

A fluttering at the base of my throat catches me off guard. I stand stock still and let myself absorb the crazy idea forming in my head. I see myself standing on a stage. An ancient Greek stage. I blink and the image disappears.

I tie back my hair. I'm imagining things. Must be the crazy heat and the island air.

I head outside for a walk. Maybe a run. Ava said the secret to overcoming jetlag is to exercise and drink plenty of water. I'm going to try a couple of laps around the olive trees.

Ajax and his father are already in the fields. Mrs. Christos looks busy on the phone in their company office next door to the house.

She waves at me from the large window looking out over the gravel driveway.

I wave back and smile. I recall that Elena is still in school as their summer starts a little later.

As soon as I step outdoors, I have to squint against the strong sunshine. It's a jolt to my system.

Portland, Maine is in the northern hemisphere of the U.S., so even in summer, our days are mostly cool and comfortable, with clouds and showers and downpours.

Here, it's an intense sun that has me scrambling for extra sunblock.

"There you are," Ajax says as he strolls up, shirtless and sweaty.

I thought he looked yummy over the phone. In person, I'm careful not to drool. His triceps have triceps.

Don't stare, Bridget. Thirsty is not a good look, as Daisy would say.

Ajax's smile makes up for all my tired achy feelings. I smile back, itching to hug him but hold myself back.

"I'm thinking of doing some laps. To wake up my body. After that long flight and good food. I need to do something."

He nods, picking up some branches off the ground and peering at the seeds or fruit or whatever is on them.

"You're welcome to join me." I eyeball his muscled torso. Not like he needs to, I think.

"Are you nuts?" Ajax laughs as I lace up my sneakers.

"Nope." I shake my head.

"It's too hot."

"It's only 8 a.m."

"The sun's been up for three hours."

"Oh," I say, feeling a bit dejected that I'm late to the party. "I wonder if I could ever do farmer hours."

A loud *harrumph* sound comes from up a tree. It sounds like

Ajax's father. Is Mr. Christos in a tree? Do they climb trees all day long? Will I have to climb trees to get the right photos for their posts?

"Good morning, Bridget." Mr. Christos's voice comes from somewhere in the branches.

"Good morning, sir," I shout to the sky.

"No sir, please call me Christos."

"Isn't that your last name?"

Ajax smiles, "The oldest Christos goes by our surname. It's tradition, for us anyway."

I look around at the wide expanse of trees. I register a mental promise to myself to do my best job ever to showcase this beautiful farm and its products.

I turn to see Ajax leaning on a tool, probably a spade, I guess. Muscles bulge out on both sides of his frame. He looks like the featured photo on a farmer's calendar.

"So, no running for you?" I ask nonchalantly. "You've been sweating for hours already," I tease. "What's a little more?"

"I still have work to do. The trees are on a schedule." He waves his hand at where his phone is sitting on top of his t-shirt next to an olive tree far down the lane.

"But . . . I'm getting more done not gripping the phone in one hand while I tell you bedtime stories." He smirks.

"Meanie," I swat his arm. "I'm leaving. Is there any area I should avoid?"

He looks like he's thinking about it. "No, not really. If you reach the fence line which is way over there," he points towards green hills, "then you've reached the end of the property."

"Seriously?" I shade my eyes. "How far is that? Like several football fields long?"

He gives me an answer in hectares which leaves me as clueless as ever.

"Okay, I'll be back."

He lowers his voice. "Shouldn't you kiss me goodbye or something?" He does a side-eye toward his father on the other side of the olive tree.

"Oh, yeah," I mutter softly. I lean forward and press my lips to his cheek. His outdoor musky scent infiltrates my nose. It's male and sexy and . . . for the next few months . . . it's mine!

A ripple of excitement races through my veins. I take another look at this hunk.

His stare is so intense I feel my bones melting under his gaze.

I swallow. "Okay . . . I'm off."

"You don't have to leave." He whispers in a tone I've never heard from him.

I look away. Time to get out of the furnace, Bridget, because you sure as heck can't stand the heat. I whip around quickly and dash off at full speed. Such a rookie move.

MY JOG IS . . . RELAXING, IF THAT'S POSSIBLE. I LOOP through the trees, my feet springing along on top of the leaf-covered ground. I inhale the scent of trees and flowers and sea salt.

I thought I'd see only olive trees. When I run past the last row of trees I end up in a wide grassy meadow. I've never had to use the word 'meadow' before. I thought those only existed in Jane Austen or Anne of Green Gables books.

But here I am on a Greek island, in a real-life meadow, with swaying grasses and wildflowers.

I pluck one flower and tie the stem into my hair.

"You're a full-blown country girl now!"

I swing around to see my fake fiancé standing there, still shirtless, sweat running in rivers down his flat stomach.

"How'd you find me?"

He gives me a look that clashes between *duh* and 'you're so adorable.' I lean toward the latter and grin. "I thought you had to work."

He plops down in the meadow.

I sink down beside him. He plucks a long piece of grass and twists it between his fingers.

"Papa said to go, he'd finish up."

My eyes open wide. "Is that good? Or bad?"

Ajax shakes his head as if he has no clue. "I'll take it as a good sign. He said I should spend your first day here with you. He's right."

"What about the trees? They need you."

He raises his dark eyes to mine. "What about you?"

I hold his look. "Me?" I whisper.

His head nods slowly up and down. Dark eyes lock on mine. His fingers have stopped twisting grass and are reaching towards my face. He slides a piece of hair away but does not break his gaze.

"Yes, Bridge, do you need me?"

I gulp.

I close my eyes and take a calming breath. I can't handle his intensity.

He drops his hand and pulls at another piece of grass. The spell is broken.

"Well, I sure need you to show me around this gorgeous island," I say heartily. "I'm thinking I'd do a montage of footage starting from the ferry dock, which I got yesterday, and ending up at the farm."

"That sounds cool," he says, shifting seamlessly from intense to casual, which I can handle better.

"Right. I wish I could get some aerial footage."

He sits up. "We have a drone, if that would work."

"What? You have a drone, and you don't use it?"

"We use it all the time to get footage of the tree tops."

"That makes sense." I leap up. I reach down a hand to pull him up. "What are we waiting for? You have a drone. This is going to be epic. I can see the images in my head already."

Ajax grins at me. "Like a travel reality show?"

"Better. An olive oil, Greek island, hot guy reality show."

He screws up his mouth. "I'm not going to be in the ads. Please!"

"Why not? We must present the product as a family brand." I point a finger at him. "And you, my dear, are the face of the brand. Oldest son, heir to the empire and all that."

He casts his eyes down to the ground. Is Ajax shy? No way!

"Hold up. You're not camera-shy, are you? With that face and those dimples?" Not to mention his hunky bod, but let's not go there again.

He raises pleading eyes to me. "Can't we use Papa? He's the patriarch."

I start walking in what I hope is the right direction. It isn't.

"Um . . . Bridget?"

"Yeah?"

I swing around to see him pointing in a different direction off to my left. "Let's go back this way. I want to show you something."

"Cool."

We walk in silence for a while. I'm busy thinking about how to present the family business with Papa as the lead, but it doesn't work in my head. Probably because I've been seeing Ajax as the face of Christos Olive Oil.

"We're here."

I focus on our surroundings. A tree as old as time sits majestically in the center of a clearing. Like a holy tree or something. "What's this one called?"

"It's our tree patriarch. The first Christos olive tree."

I stop walking and stare. "It's . . ." I'm not sure how to describe it. Gnarled roots twist and turn like hands over hands over hands, all joined and strong. Usually, trees have a nice trunk — you can tell where it starts and where the roots go. But this old tree has roots and trunk all mashed together.

"This guy looks strong as hell."

Ajax grins. "Meet Tobias."

"He has a name?"

"Well, that was the name of my and Elena's great-grandfather who planted it 200 years ago."

I grab my phone and begin taking a video of Tobias, walking around it, or him, to get its strong, silent, commanding beauty from all angles.

"I'll start with the tree patriarch," I tell Ajax slipping my phone back into my pocket.

He nods. "Good idea."

"Plus, he's much more handsome than you are."

"I think so," Ajax agrees easily, no humor in his voice. Just pure reverence. It makes me look at Tobias again.

I try to see what Ajax sees in this tree. It's old. It's kind of ugly. But it's been here for a long, long time.

Maybe that's its beauty. It's withstood a lot and is still standing.

A potential new logo for the company forms in my head.

"Are you ready?" Ajax asks.

I nod. "Yeah, we can come back here, right?"

"Of course, Bridge, anytime." The way he smiles at me, it's like I passed a test I didn't know I was taking.

But that's fine. As long as I passed.

Our walk back is slow, meandering through the trees as he explains the whats and whys of olive farming. It's a lot to take in at once but I'm starting to see why he loves it.

"The olive branch is the symbol of peace and hope," Ajax says, fingering the branches as if they are friends whose hands he's shaking.

"And friendship," I add. "I looked it up."

"Right," he says thoughtfully. "Friendship."

Is it me or was there a smidge of disappointment in his voice just then?

I spin around, arms wide open. "I love it here, Ajax. More than I imagined." Which is true.

"You haven't even seen the beach yet." He laughs.

I stop spinning and put my hands on my hips. "What are we waiting for?"

"Let's go!" He grabs me and throws me over his shoulder.

The world is upside down, but I don't care. I'm being transported through a woodland paradise by a man who takes my breath away. In more ways than one.

Chapter Twenty-Five

AJAX

As I wait for Bridget to finish getting ready to go on our island tour, I wash down the Jeep and vacuum up olive leaves scattered on the floormats.

I've already secured the drone in the back seat. My heart is racing at the idea of spending the entire day with her.

Picking her up and carrying her to the house surprised me. Like I'm looking for ways to hold her.

I've got to stop with my longing looks and verbal innuendoes. I don't want to scare her away. And I don't want to make her feel uncomfortable either.

I must remember I only have one summer with her. I want it to be perfect. I don't want to come across creepy and grabby.

Although I already know she's the only woman for me. She's perfection. I need to appreciate she's here to help my family — and me. I need to stop trying to make it more than it is.

It's my body that forgets the mission and operates all on its own.

What a dude! I mutter to myself. I cringe inside thinking back to how I stared at her in the fields, as if I was a vampire intent on drinking her blood or something.

Be a friend, not a fanatic.

"What are you brooding about big brother?" Elena appears up the driveway. The school bus leaves her off at the gate and she must have skipped up without me even noticing, that's how deep in my head I am.

"I'm not brooding. How do you even know that word?"

"TV," she smirks at me. "And yes, you were being all moony-eyed."

I snort. "You mean cow-eyed."

She frowns. "No bro, I'm pretty sure they call it moon eyes. Anyways, whatever it's called, you got it bad. I'm so glad she loves you back."

I stop wiping down the wax on the hood of the Jeep. "What do you know? Has she said something to you?"

She steps backward. "Whoa! Slow down. What do you mean what do *I* know?" A frown creases her little forehead. "Is there something I *should* know?"

I focus on swishing my cloth around as fast as possible on the hood.

But Elena doesn't leave it alone. "What are you hiding?"

"Nothing," I mutter. "Nothing at all."

What a lie. I'm hiding my deep feelings for the girl who flew thousands of miles here to help me and my family.

That's what those romantic movies call a grand gesture. Except Bridget didn't do it out of love for me. She did it because she's a good friend.

Elena is still staring with a perplexed frown when Bridget comes outside looking stunning in a white sleeveless top and cream-colored shorts. Her legs are as toned as her arms, the results of her daily runs and workouts, I guess.

"Your tongue is hanging out, bro," Elena laughs.

I close my mouth and glare at Elena. "Thanks a lot. You can go now."

She folds her arms squarely across her body and fixes me with a smile that could sink a ship. "Hi, Bridget," Elena says sweeter than honey. "What are you and my brother up to today?"

Bridget greets Elena with a hug.

Elena breaks her stance and drops her arms. Her entire body melts into Bridget's as they hug. Something I wish I could do on the regular.

Bridget eyes me over Elena's head. "Can she come with us?"

I manage to stifle my groan. Is it selfish that I want her all to myself? At least today.

Elena reads people better than she reads words. It's like her secret weapon. "No, thank you. I've got homework. But Ajax will show you all my favorite places, won't you?"

I nod, afraid to speak up. I swear my little sister runs me like I'm a train and she's the conductor.

"Right, big brother?"

"Right."

"Okay, you two lovebirds. Enjoy." Elena's sharp glance travels between me and Bridget then back to me again. Her eyes soften as she tilts her head. Like she's noticing something. And it's making her sad for me.

Chapter Twenty-Six

AJAX

"Little sisters are the same all over the world, I see," Bridget says as she straps on her seat belt and settles her feet on the clean mats.

I'm happy to see she's wearing hiking sandals. Because where we're going, there'll be dirt and rocks and sand and all sorts of outdoor terrain.

"What do you mean?" I ask steering us along the quiet roadways toward the Temple of Aphaia.

"I mean they love to be in the know. They long to be a part of our lives and they don't like being left out."

"Oh. I guess. I never thought about Elena as being needy at all. She's so independent. With a hell of a lot more confidence than most people have at any age."

Bridget looks around out the windows. After a while she says, "I hope nothing happens for her to lose that confidence and joy."

My heart almost stops. Bridget must be thinking back to when she was Elena's age. At twelve, her own mother was dying of cancer. Nothing must have been joyful back then.

I wonder how it affected her. Did she lose confidence in herself? Or did it affect her in a different way?

"I hope not, too," I say, reaching across for her hand. She puts her hand in mine, and I feel her smooth cool palm under my rough callused one. It fits perfectly.

We drive for a bit in silence until we get to the top of the hill close to the temple. I don't give any information about where we're going.

I park the car next to two other vehicles in the almost empty gravel lot. We walk side by side up the concrete steps, glittering like they were poured with diamonds in their mix.

"Where's the temple?" Bridget asks pointing to the sign announcing we're at the ancient Temple of Aphaia. She looks around. "Is it those rocks there?" She points to centuries-old bits of leftover wall that once surrounded the temple.

"We're not there as yet."

The sound of the cicadas is so loud, it's almost deafening. The trees and insects are alive here. I wonder if she notices them. She must. It's like an outdoor concert of sounds.

Then above the cicadas, I hear her intake of breath.

"Oh, my goodness, Ajax."

We've walked past the steps and through the pathway of trees.

"This is . . ." She's lost her words. I grin to myself. A feeling of joy fills me up to know I've made her speechless with wonder.

She turns wide eyes toward me and throws her arms around my neck. "This is the most beautiful thing I've ever seen in my life."

She steps back and points. "It's a real temple. Like what you see in movies. It's right here in your backyard. This is amazing."

I agree with her there. We may be different in many ways, but one thing is clear. We both know what we love, and we love it wholly and completely. Her passion equals mine.

"The Temple of Aphaia has seen better days back in 500 B.C., that's for sure," I tell her. "But it always takes my breath away no matter how often I come here."

Like you, Bridget Walker, except I don't say that aloud.

"I feel like I should be wearing a toga and laurel leaves on my head as I stroll up to this . . . ," she stops speaking.

"Sanctuary?"

"Yes, that's the word I was looking for." She smiles. "Thank you."

We walk around the temple's perimeter, getting as close as we can to the columns, but still staying at a respectable distance.

"If you close one eye, you can imagine how glorious this building looked with all its columns intact. And people roaming around it."

Bridget smacks one hand over her right eye and stares at the columns, a smile breaking across her lips.

"Looks like the kind of structure you'd build in a major destination, not on this little goat island." Bridget's face is glowing in the sunshine.

I bend down to pick up a cone from one of the many pine trees dotting the hill and sniff the rich piney scent. I offer it to Bridget who takes it as if it's a priceless gift.

"It smells amazing up here, all these pine trees and the breeze wafting through the columns."

Bridget doesn't answer. She's busy snapping photos of the broken stone slabs on the ground that once fit neatly into the massive structure.

"I like this better than the Parthenon," she says.

"You haven't seen the Parthenon yet," I laugh. "But we'll take the ferry to Athens to visit Athena's famous site."

"I like that we have this temple to ourselves. No crowds."

I have to agree.

"This place is cool and quiet, and you can imagine ancient Aegina citizens wandering around or sitting outside on the stone steps talking philosophy and physics. Or myths and magic. Or art and religion."

Her face gets wistful.

"What's wrong?"

She sighs and keeps walking, picking her way through the gravel and rocks.

"I think my mother would have loved this so much. She would have painted it. She painted, you know. Murals and stuff. I forget that sometimes. I forget she painted. I feel like I'm forgetting her but then I come here, and I can see her clearly."

I want to go to Bridget and wrap her in my arms and make the day, the world better for her. But all I can do is listen.

"I find that when I come to the temple or to my other favorite place on the island, the olive sanctuary, I feel life more deeply," I share.

"I think they call those vibrations." She picks her away around another edge of the temple.

"Maybe," I tilt my head at her. "I'm not well-versed in that stuff. I only know how I feel."

"I feel it, too. Here." She smiles gently at me. "I can hear the voices of the centuries."

"Let's go down there," I point to a flight of steps leading downwards to dark doors.

"Sketchy."

"It's a museum."

"It's deserted. And underground. Like a tomb."

"I'll protect you. We'll uncover the Temple of Aphaia's mysteries."

"You're so weird!"

"Same as you."

Inside, a low ceiling and few windows give the room a dim cave-like feeling.

"Have you been here before?" she asks, her voice trembling.

I take her hand. It feels so natural. "It's a legit museum, I promise."

We stop in front of a statue of a Greek man squatting on his heels, one arm outstretched with a closed fist. Other bronze statutes hang about as they've been doing for centuries.

"Dude!" Bridget's eyes open wide. "What are these?"

"From the original temple. A lot of the most valuable pieces were taken by the Germans and sit in a museum in Munich." I say that bitterly as it's an old beef. But I sweep my hand outward to showcase what we do have left.

"Ta da!"

Bridget thrusts her phone into my hands an excited look on her face. "Take my picture." She stretches out one arm and pretends to give the ancient marble man a fist bump.

"Yes, madam."

Bridget takes off her backpack and carries it by her fingers. "I don't want to knock over anything," she explains. "It's crazy there're no guards following us around making sure we don't damage anything?"

"It's called trust and respect."

She smirks at me. "Let's take a selfie."

We pose together, heads close, next to a classic Greek statue with a head full of tangled curls.

A glass case filled with gold ornaments catches Bridget's eye. She points to a pair of ancient dangly earrings.

"Those remind me of my mother."

I stop walking and face Bridget. "What was her name?"

"Hazel. She was awesome." The sadness in Bridget's voice stabs at my heart.

"I'm so sorry you lost her."

"Me, too. But you know what the worst part is?"

"I can't imagine," I say honestly.

Bridget turns tearful eyes on me. "I didn't spend time with her when she was sick. I was too busy with my dance and song lessons following this dumb dream of being an actress."

"Oh, honey," I murmur, gathering her into my arms. "I didn't know your mom, but I bet she was proud of you for following your dream."

"I thought she'd be in the audience when I got my chance to perform. I never imagined she wouldn't be. I didn't believe the cancer was stronger than she was."

She snuffles close to my chest, and I stroke her back. Maybe it's because we're on ancient sacred ground that the entire outside world falls aside. There's no space here for anything but truth.

"I was an actor in every school play and musical. From high school straight to college. Until my junior year at college when I just stopped."

"Why?" I whisper, nuzzling the top of her head.

"I was chasing something I could never catch."

I kiss her forehead and close my eyes. I try to imagine what my life would be like without my mother or my father. Impossible.

"I could never ever find peace." She sighs as if a weight is holding her down.

"How do you feel after giving up acting?"

She steps away from me and looks around the museum. "I feel like these," she says, pointing at the ancient artifacts. "Broken."

I shake my head hard. "They're beautiful. Flawed. And still perfect."

"Why are they still perfect?"

"Because that's how they were created. And neither time, nor events, nor the trial of life changes their true nature."

She tugs at one of her curls. "You're talking about them? Or me?"

"Both," I say firmly.

Chapter Twenty-Seven

BRIDGET

After our moment in the underground museum, I feel closer to Ajax than to anyone on the planet, including my sisters.

Now he knows the truth about me. I didn't spend time with my mother the year before she died because I was selfish. Following a dream.

I've never shared my deep regrets about Mom. Not with anyone.

I don't know what it means that I shared this with Ajax. But it *feels* like I gave a piece of my frozen heart to him to thaw out and protect.

"We have much more to see on Aegina," Ajax says with as much positivity as he can muster, given my underground revelations.

We climb back into his Jeep and keep driving.

Nothing on Aegina is what I expected, or like what I read about.

I expected beauty, sure, but the empty roads and towering pine trees, the craggy mountains and the thousands of little chapels everywhere are capturing my heart and soul. The island is weaving a spell around me with its calming energy.

Maybe I feel free to share with Ajax the things I keep hidden back home because of this magical island.

Or maybe it's because Ajax values his family as much as I care about mine. Which is obvious in how he respects his little sister Elena.

And his parents. Agreeing immediately with me to fund our fake engagement party so they wouldn't have that expense.

Seeing him and Elena interact warms me toward Ajax in ways that talking on the phone for months couldn't accomplish.

Although I earn a living creating remote connections to products and people, this in-person contact is unbeatable.

I can look into his eyes. Feel his rough hands. Hear his caring voice and match his tone with his body language.

I feel as if I've walked through a black-and-white world into a full color one, like Dorothy in *The Wizard of Oz*.

The last part of our day is dedicated to a hike Ajax promised will be spectacular.

I try to ignore the stabbing pain of blisters growing across my instep from the velcro clasps. My hiking sandals are rubbing them raw.

He's too excited leading the way amongst the endless bushes and rocks for me to complain.

This part of Aegina is arid. Cacti of all shapes and sizes dot the ground cover.

"Are you leading me into a remote location far from civilization? You know my sisters all have me on speed dial while I'm in Greece. Not to mention, they also have your phone number and a photo. You can't get rid of me no matter how annoying I am."

Ajax scoffs. "You're not annoying. You're a lightweight in the annoying department."

"Cool," I say, forcing a smile. "I was holding back."

His grin turns to a frown. "Are you tired?"

I guess he sees the expression of pain dotting my face.

I shake my head and point at my sandals. "It's these suckers. They're killing me."

He frowns and walks over, stepping around the cacti like they're made of gold.

"I'm wearing these trekking sandals for the first time and they're not as comfortable as the ads said!"

He leads me to a large boulder and settles me down by pushing gently on my shoulders before raising one of my feet.

"May I?" he asks raising his deep dark eyes to mine.

I nod. Thank God I had a pedicure before I came. My feet may hurt but they look their best!

He unstraps the Velcro strap across my instep and I tense up. He's staring in my eyes as he slowly removes my sandal. Like I'm as precious as the cacti.

I do my best to focus on not showing it's hurting. But it is.

And when he removes the sandal completely, we see why. An angry red welt of flesh is uncovered. So much for cute feet.

He does the same to the other sandal and yep, another crimson welt like I was hit with a whip on my feet.

"And I think I've got blisters on my heels, too," I add sorrowfully.

He sits back on his haunches. "How long has this been hurting you, Bridget?"

I shrug. "Awhile."

He stares me down.

"Since the temple. I've never worn hiking sandals before. I have hiking boots back home. That's standard in Maine. But I thought they'd be inappropriate for an island, so I went with these." I hold up one of the cute shoes that I thought would go with everything from shorts to long swishy skirts.

Not!

He opens his mouth to say something, then closes it again.

Opening his backpack, he pulls at a zip lock bag of band aids and other first aid items.

I flinch as he pours water on my feet and takes off his t-shirt to wipe them down.

Is this man for real?

He's washing my feet!

I'm in such shock, I stare speechless.

He expertly rips open a band aid between his teeth and squeezes out some kind of soothing cream onto the red welts. Then he bandages them and leans back.

"That should ease the pain a bit. But you can't wear these shoes again today."

We stare into each other's eyes.

I glance around at the rocky dirt full of sharp pebbles and stones and roots and CACTI!

"Um . . ."

He packs his bag and slides it to his front. Then he scoots down to my level. I'm still sitting so he's basically backing up his entire body next to mine.

"Get on."

"What?"

"It's the only way you're making it out of here without killing your feet."

I gulp. "You want me to ride on your back? For *milessss*??!!"

The last part is a screech and he turns around with a massive grin. "Geez, Bridge, I never took you for squeamish."

"I never had to walk through a desert barefoot before."

He pats my knees. "Climb up, my city girl. I'll carry you. It's not like we have a choice."

I look at the sandals he's strapped to the outside of his backpack. "Yeah, I never want to put those on again!"

He chuckles. "We can get you some flip flops in town. Or whatever you like. We have lots of cute shops. Nothing like a big city, but pretty good."

I bite my lip. I don't care about flip flops or cute shops. I care that I may be too heavy for him, and he'll hurt himself carrying me around like a sack of potatoes.

"What's wrong?" he turns around again when I fail to clamber aboard Train Ajax.

"I'm considering walking."

He eyes me, patience in his eyes.

He scrubs his chin with his hands and his eyes look downward, his smirk gone.

"I know it's not ideal having to hold on to me for long, but I promise, it's platonic. I know you don't see me as a romantic guy, like in movies and books."

"What kind of guy?"

"The ones who carry their girlfriends on their backs, looking all happy and in love."

"Oh," I nod sagely. "Right. I don't hold much stock in those scenes. They're usually posed. They're not even real couples."

"Like us," he mumbles.

I catch it though. His words might not have been meant for my ears, but I heard them. I also hear a strange longing in what he doesn't say.

Does Ajax *like me* like me? No way. We're just friends.

And what if he liked me as more than a friend? What would happen then?

I gulp. In theory it sounds amazing.

But in reality, it couldn't possibly work. Could it?

Before I could continue down that rabbit hole, I stand up gingerly on my bare feet and take a giant leap to get on his back.

He grabs my legs like I weigh nothing and hoists me higher up so that my entire body is leaning on his back.

His warmth seeps through me. His maleness is almost overpowering in close proximity.

I've had my share of boyfriends. But I've never dated a man. A man like Ajax anyway.

And although we're just faking it, right now, as I lean on him, my legs wrapped around his waist, his arms scooped under them, this is the closest I've ever gotten to a real-life romance.

The grin on his face is catching.

"Giddy up horsey," I say, pulling on his curls gently.

"Don't go there," he teases, "I'll run, and you won't like it."

"I don't know. I thought I wouldn't like this, but I think I could get used to it."

"Oh, really?" he says. "I think I could too."

My heart jolts straight to my throat.

A vision of us doing this every day — well, not *every* single day — flashes through my mind. A vision of me and Ajax sailing off on that sailboat together into the sunset flickers for the briefest moment.

"What're you thinking about? You're so quiet back there."

I shake my head to return to the moment. "Nothing."

I kiss the back of his head. For no reason other than that I am grateful this guy cares about me so much he's lugging my big butt around a desert.

Chapter Twenty-Eight

BRIDGET

Our hike continues for almost half an hour. Well, he hikes, I cling.

Like a koala bear or a little furry sloth.

Every ten minutes he readjusts me, hoisting me higher as I start to slip down. My bandaged feet dangle like the useless limbs they are right now.

"You know this is ridiculous, right?" I tell him. "We should have gone back to the Jeep. Now you have to carry me all the way back."

He doesn't answer. Probably because he's conserving his energy to hoist my butt to some unknown destination that he swears I will love.

"Hun, you're going to be exhausted. Make this make sense please."

Then he steps out from the scrubs and through a pine grove and there before us, is the prize.

And it's worth it!

"You've got to be kidding me!" I say, sliding down from his back and letting my feet sink into the softest sand.

He lets out a giant sigh and stands up straight stretching his arms above his head.

"Are you okay?"

"I carry trees, Bridget. When they're dead or when I've pruned their branches off and can't get the tractor close. Whole trees sometimes."

"I get it. You're strong."

He grins. "Welcome to my private oasis."

He sweeps one arm outward. I gawk at the shimmering turquoise sea. Even standing from twenty yards away, I can see right to the seabed, where pink sand meets pink rocks.

"What is this place?" I ask. "Are we even on the same island? And dude, you could have started with this! I'd have never left."

"Exactly." He pulls his soaking wet t-shirt over his head, muscles bulging all over the place, except now I appreciate them for their functional use, not just their aesthetics.

"You coming?" He gives me no time to respond before he races into the blue water.

Drops splash back on me and I shiver. "What are we supposed to do with these?" I raise up a foot and point to a bandage.

"You can take those off. I just covered them while we trekked through the desert."

I unpeel the bandages and examine my feet.

"I'll live!" I shout.

His head is under the water so he doesn't hear me.

I'm wearing my swimsuit under my clothes so I pull off my shorts and shirt, folding them carefully into a bundle and resting them on the top of his backpack. His clothing is strewn all about the rocks.

"Come on in," he invites, popping back up. He looks like Poseidon himself.

He dives under and pops up again, his dark curls sleeked back on his head. Drops of water shimmer on his broad shoulders as he walks toward me.

I dip one toe in, then another. "It's so warm!" I exclaim. I'm used to swimming in the chilly waters of the North Atlantic. This right here is not just the element of water, it's air and earth and water and fire combined. It's all of them at once.

By the time my brain has given the green light to the rest of my body to dive in, Ajax is standing right in front of me.

"Get back," I shout. "I'm taking my time."

"Woman, you're too slow."

Part of me wishes he would submerge himself. I can't handle all the yummy hotness he's exuding.

I close my eyes when I get to my waist and dive in. The water feels like a thousand kisses on my skin, smooth and sweet and caressing.

I swim underwater until I feel my lungs crying and I pop up, shaking the hair and drops of water out of my eyes.

Ajax is floating on his back right near me.

"This is the best thing I've ever experienced in my life."

He raises an eyebrow. "Really?"

"Yes, really," I say. "Not all of us live on a beautiful Greek island."

He grins. "Well, you're here now. Surrounded by the sea. And the mountains. And the trees . . ."

"And you." I dive under as soon as I say those words. I swim towards the pink rocks.

Ajax passes me with a few strong strokes. I tread water, gazing at the flat rocks that jut into the cove. He pulls himself up and beckons me to follow.

When I manage to hoist myself up with his help, we lean back on our elbows side by side. Sea water drips off my skin in rivulets.

Ajax leans over and slides a rough finger along my arm, stopping a trail of water and flicking it away.

"Thanks," I breathe in a husky voice. His nearness is making me tremble.

"You cold?" he asks softly.

I shake my head no. The heat of the sun has nothing on Ajax's overpowering fire. Everything about him screams masculine energy. He makes me feel protected and adored and something else.

"What're you thinking about?" he asks, flicking another drop of water off my burning skin.

No one is around. There're no human sounds even when I strain my ears to try and hear traffic or people talking.

"This is pretty isolated, huh?" I whisper.

He nods slowly. "Completely isolated."

"Great." I swallow. "Then no one will see this." I lean over and without a thought at all as to what it means or how to come back from it, I press my mouth on my best friend's lips.

The moment our lips touch, I feel and hear explosions behind my closed eyelids.

Ajax swoops me onto his lap, pressing my head backward so it's him kissing me now.

I wasn't expecting that. All coherent thoughts leave me completely. I am nothing but sunlight, seawater, and Ajax's tantalizing mouth.

His lips slide along my collarbone. Parts of me I didn't know could tremble with excitement are ignited under his touch.

My very soul is welcoming him. As if I've been waiting for him all my life.

The air hums with insects. The trees wave their branches above us and Ajax's fingers find mine. Our hands lock together as one.

I don't think anything could have prepared me for the feeling of peace that invades my soul.

This feeling that everything will be okay. And that this man holding me, kissing me, is a big reason why.

I close my eyes and float into it.

With Ajax's strong hand clasped tightly in my own, I won't float too far away from him.

Chapter Twenty-Nine

AJAX

Nothing in my life will ever be the same.

I don't care what anyone thinks. I've found my soul-mate in Bridget Walker.

Except she doesn't know it. Or won't admit it.

As soon as I raise my head from kissing her sweet lips, she blinks at me in confusion. Like she can't believe what she did.

And I, not wanting to lose this precious moment, make the biggest mistake.

"I love you, Bridget," I say it with the utter conviction I feel in my heart and soul. "I love you," I repeat, in case she didn't hear me the first time.

"Um . . ." she hesitates. I slide her to a sitting position and release my arm from around her shoulders. I wait patiently for her to respond.

The rock I'm leaning against digs into my shoulder. It doesn't feel anything like the pain I'm experiencing in my heart at her silence.

The sun hides behind a cloud as if it's embarrassed for me.

The silence is worse than if she'd just laugh. She stares toward the pebbly beach, then shifts her body to look out toward the horizon.

"Say something," I beg, like a man with no pride.

I don't care. Everything's changed. The dream of Bridget has become a reality and I refuse to lose this new reality.

It's the best thing that's ever happened to me in my life. I've dated a lot of women in college, but never have I been mesmerized by anyone until Bridget. It's not just her beauty, which is obvious. It's her wide-open heart always ready to help others.

She glances over her shoulder at me, like she can't face me. "I'm sorry, Ajax. I don't know what to say. I shouldn't have kissed you so impulsively."

My heart teeter-totters right off the edge of the rock.

Her body swings around to face mine. She crosses her legs resting her palms up like she's about to start a yoga class. "It's not that I can't see us together."

My heart flutters. "But?"

Her dark eyes look sad. "You live here." She cast her arms wide like she's gathering up the shimmering sea, pink sand, and the setting sun. Throwing them into my face.

"Right?"

She shrugs her shoulders. "And I don't."

I brush damp curls off her shoulders. I'm pitiful. Anything to touch her. My heart is screaming, make her understand. Make her see how much you love her.

"Do you think you could ever love me?" I ask.

"I already love you, Ajax."

"No, I mean as a boyfriend . . . or a real fiancé?"

She swallows. Her eyes blink hard as if trying to stop the truth from escaping their depths.

"Nevermind. It's okay. I'm glad you love me, however you do. Let's go home."

Who am I to pour my feelings on her so fast, demanding answers?

"I'm sorry," I tell her as we clamber down the rocks toward the pebbly beach. "I have no right to make a big deal out of a kiss."

Her lips slide upwards a tiny bit. "It was a great kiss."

I smile back at her, my lips remembering the feel of hers under them. "It was."

THE BEST PART OF HAVING BRIDGET ON AEGINA IS THAT she's always near me if I want to tell her something. Or if I want to reach out and touch her arm or grab her in a quick hug.

I bury the memory of our first (and only) kiss in the back of my mind. Better to focus on what I have than what I don't have. That's the secret to happiness, I've been told.

After our first day of sightseeing, I feel closer to her than I ever did before. We crossed a barrier of some kind. And not just because of our intimate kiss. It started when she confided in me at the Temple of Aphaia about losing her mom.

I could feel her anguish. She still carries it deep within her. I wish there was something I could do to ease that pain.

It's been more than ten years, but Bridget seems stuck in her 13-year-old mind where her mother's death is concerned. As if she can't escape that tragedy.

The next morning, we get Papa and Mama together on the patio and thank them for their offer but explain our plan to host the engagement party ourselves.

Papa is drinking a cup of coffee. He glances at Mama.

Mama asks, "Are you sure?"

Bridget and I reach for each other's hands automatically. "We're sure," we say in unison.

Papa nods his head while rubbing his chin. "Is this how they do it in America? The kids plan their own celebrations?"

"Sometimes," Bridget says.

"Okay for us," Papa responds, nodding at Mama.

We all agree that six weeks is enough time for me and Bridget to organize the festivities.

Bridget asks Mama for a list of email addresses to send out invites online.

"I'm happy to see you two are taking control of your destiny. Character is destiny, as you know."

"He's quoting a famous Greek philosopher. I can't recall which one," I say to Bridget.

"What does it mean though?" Bridget whispers to me.

I shrug.

Papa throws up his hands. "It means your character, who you are, will determine your destiny, it is not a predetermined outside force. And you two are showing strength of character. So maybe . . .," he doesn't finish but he waggles his eyebrows at us.

"Papa, we're planning a party, not preparing to sack Troy."

"Your name is Ajax. Live up to it."

"Yes, sir."

"And you," he turns toward my fiancée. "Your name . . ."

"Yes?" she asks hesitantly.

"It means strength and power."

Bridget and I give each other wide-eyed looks.

"Thanks," she says, raising her voice. Channeling some of that strength.

"Six weeks may be plenty of time for you two to organize your own party. But don't forget, we have a lot of work to do here. The farm comes first."

"Of course, it does," I try not to let any sarcasm seep through.

I love the farm; it comes first for the family. But right now, Bridget also comes first. It's a tie.

"I'll be working on the marketing plan during that time, Mr. Christos."

"Christos. Just Christos," he mutters as he walks off.

"Does he even like me?" Bridget asks, her voice trembling a bit.

I scoff. "He loves you."

"How do you know that? He barely looks at me and he reminded me my name means strength. Like he wants me to show some."

I cuddle her near me. Her sunglasses, which are perched on her forehead, almost fall off and I catch them in one hand.

"Trust me, he likes you. But you know what? Tonight, after dinner, we'll do something he loves to do. I've found that the best way to connect with my father is to play his game. Literally."

"What do you mean?"

"We're going to beat him at ping pong."

Bridget giggles. "Beat him at what he enjoys? That doesn't sound like a winning plan."

"Trust me, he loves ping pong. I'll call up his brother and we'll challenge the Christos brothers to a duel tonight after dinner. Playing a game is the best way to get to know anyone. It's the whole essence of being Greek."

She wrinkles up her forehead. "Oh really? Why?"

I kiss the tip of her nose. It comes naturally and I pull back, holding my breath to see if she'll object. When she doesn't, I assume she accepts it as part of my affectionate nature.

"We invented the ultimate game."

"I thought it was the Japanese who invented Nintendo?"

This time I laugh out loud. "I'm talking about the Olympics. The ultimate sporting event."

"Ah! Pulling rank on cultural grounds. Well, my dear, ancient Africans invented baseball, so there."

"Really, tell me more."

She explains all about a game called "*ta kurt om el mahag*" that ancient Libyans played in the desert with the same, or similar, rules to baseball.

I nod in appreciation to my mini history lesson.

She ends with, "Anyway, how do you know if I'm any good at ping pong? I could suck at it, and he'd see me as a loser. Or weak or something else lacking for Greeks."

I almost double over laughing. "Geez woman, it's a game. He's not going to disown you. Neither will I. Anyway, you already told me you play ping pong a lot with your sisters back home. So . . ."

"You remember."

"I remember everything you tell me."

She stares deeply into my eyes as if trying to discern whether it's true.

I blink. "I have a very good memory." My voice falters.

"Oh, that's cool. Okay, ping pong later. We should do some practice rounds."

I promise her we will.

Papa and I head outside to the trees while Bridget continues working on her laptop.

Between the remote work she's doing for her publishing client, and the marketing plan she's creating for our olive oil, she's busier than I am.

I offer to help but she insists on keeping the marketing plan a secret from everyone. Even me.

She wants to reveal it at the engagement party in front of the entire family. So the party is for a bigger purpose than just our super fake engagement.

<h1 style="text-align:center">Chapter Thirty</h1>

AJAX

"How did I not know you were a ping pong beast?" I ask incredulously, as Bridget slams another point against Papa and annihilates him.

Sweat beads on her forehead. Her face is flushed and her hands twitch as she grips her racket, ready for more.

Papa side-eyes me. "You could have warned me."

I laugh. "I had no idea."

Bridget isn't laughing. Her face is pure concentration.

"Better it's you, Papa, than me."

"Right, can't let a little girlie beat you Ajax?" Elena's laugh tinkles through the room.

My sister and I are on the sidelines enjoying the battle between Papa and Bridget that's been going on now for half an hour. Ever since Uncle Theo left and we decided to play singles.

Bridget slams the ping pong ball back continuing a lobby between her and Papa for a full couple of minutes. Papa smacks it back to her.

The ball ricochets off the end of the table and smacks Bridget right in the middle of her forehead.

"Ouch!" she says rubbing her head. I try to step in to stop the slaughter. Except I'm not sure who I'm defending, Papa or Bridget.

"Sit down," Papa growls at me.

"Bridge, are you okay?"

She's shaking her shoulders like she's ready to enter the ring again. "I'm fine, sweetheart."

I sit down fast as the game continues. I sure don't want to get in the middle of their face off.

"It's supposed to be a family game night," Mama says, coming in with glasses of freshly-squeezed lemonade. One glance from Papa, and Mama sits next to me meekly.

"I guess we're stuck here," she sighs.

Elena giggles, "I'm betting on Bridget."

Mama smiles at her. "You give up on your Papa so quickly. I'm sticking with family."

"Bridget *is* family," Elena corrects her.

Mama nods. "You're right, she is. Okay, then my bets are on Bridget, my new soon-to-be daughter-in-law. What about you, Ajax? Are you betting on your father or your fiancée?"

I gulp.

"He's Team Bridget, Mama. All the way."

"Yeah, what Elena said," I mutter watching my fake fiancée sweating it out with my father.

There's a lot of stuff I don't know about her, I'm realizing. Like that she's a killer competitor. Which is a great thing to have on my side.

It makes me wonder though, what else don't I know about her? And should I be concerned?

At that moment, Bridget turns and showers me with a dazzling smile.

My heart stumbles. Okay, I guess I can find out along the way. Isn't that what I'd be doing in an arranged marriage anyway?

"I finally got your nickname," I laugh, as Bridget devastates Papa with a backhand that sends the tiny ball spinning.

"Wow! She's full of surprises, isn't she?" Mama beams at me.

Papa looks shaken up. "I thought you were a sweet American girl," he grumbles, wiping sweat off his forehead.

She grins devilishly at him. "You should see me play against my sisters. It's a massacre."

"What's my nickname?" Bridget claws at the ball with her racket. She slides from one end of the table to the other, her racket always ready, her wrist action smooth and deliberate.

"Take that Bridget!" Papa shouts merrily as he sends a spinning ball across the net. No way she can return that. He'll finally win a game against her.

But no! Somehow, Bridget gets her racket under the ball. Like she's scooping up a ball of ice cream, she cradles it for a second and then wham! The ball flies straight toward the edge of Papa's side of the table. It hits and flies into the air above Papa's head.

"I'm going to call you *Pong*!" I laugh.

At the same time, Elena yells, "Game Bridget!"

Papa slams down his racket on top of the table and steps back. "Are you cheating?"

She freezes.

"Papa," I say. "You're being a sore loser."

"How would I cheat?" Bridget murmurs in distress.

Papa mumbles something about the table being crooked, or the rackets warped.

Mama hands Papa a glass of lemonade to calm him down. Elena scratches another winning line on the blackboard for Bridget. It's her third win over Papa.

Papa resumes his position at the table. Is he serious?

I get up from my stool. It's time to protect Bridget.

She seems oblivious to Papa's determination to win one game against her even if we stay here all night.

He's never lost a ping-pong game to anyone. I certainly didn't imagine my own fake fiancée would take him down. It's like the gods are punishing him for trying to marry me off.

Bridget slides up to me, sweat rolling down the sides of her face.

"You look hot," I whisper.

She grimaces. "I am hot." She twists her hair up into a massive bun on top her head.

"I meant like hot hot," I wink. "Watching you play is exciting."

She whips me with her racket. "Shhhh. Your parents will hear you."

"Nah, Papa's over there licking his wounds."

"I think this was a bad idea, dude. Your dad hates me more than ever now."

I nod my head. "You may be right."

Bridget gasps. "I was hoping you'd say I was wrong."

"You're annihilating him," I laugh.

She blinks slowly. "*Now* you tell me he's not a good loser. This was your idea, Ajax. What should I do?"

I wrap my arms around her shoulders and lean her backward onto my chest. "Tell him you're tired. But then he'll probably challenge you again tomorrow."

Papa and Elena appear with the ball. Elena's eyes are wide from watching Papa swear under his breath and slam his racket around.

"Mr. Christos . . . I mean, Christos," Bridget's voice falters. "I'm tired. Can Ajax take over for me, please? You wore me down."

"Are you giving up?" Papa's eyes pierce her as sharp as arrows.

I step in front of Bridget. "She's tired. We have a long day tomorrow."

Papa's mouth droops. "I was having fun."

My head swivels fast between Papa and Bridget. "You were? Looked like you were getting upset because she was winning."

Papa grins. "That's the American poker face. No?"

"Actually, Papa, a poker face means you show no emotions at all. So people don't know what you're thinking."

Papa points to his furrowed drawn-in brows and his killer eyes. "So, what's this?"

"Scary," Elena says.

We all laugh. Bridget visibly relaxes. "You're a great player, Christos. The best I've ever encountered."

He holds out a hand to shake hers, smiling broadly. "Welcome to the family, Bridget Walker. You're strong and fast and I think you possess some kind of power in your hands because they move, and I don't see them moving."

Elena, who is putting away the rackets and balls, glances at Bridget's hands hopefully. "Do you have magical hands?" she asks.

Bridget shakes her head. "Just boring, ordinary hands."

I take one of her boring, ordinary hands in mine and lead her to the arched doorway. "See you guys tomorrow."

Chapter Thirty-One

BRIDGET

Every day I wake up excited to see Ajax. It's eerie how quickly I've gotten used to being around him. We settle into a routine of early morning jogs to the meadow, then espressos under the olive trees closest to the house, picnic style.

Afterward, we split up so he can work in the fields with his father and their employees, who are mostly cousins, while I work on my laptop.

Later in the afternoons we head out in his Jeep for more sightseeing around Aegina. I've slotted myself perfectly into his world.

It makes me wonder what my own world is. Do I have one? Outside of being a sister, that is.

My job is not me; I already know that.

I enjoy marketing books, and now olive oil, but it's not what people call their *passion*. The thing they wake up excited to do every day. Like how Ajax wakes up thinking of his olive trees.

The *Sunset* book haunts me with its pressing advice to know myself. *Your greatest power is knowing yourself.*

This is why one morning I wake up and instead of following the usual routine with Ajax, I head down the long driveway and out the front gates of Christos Farm to catch a bus to town.

I've reserved a scooter at a rental agency.

Ajax stands forlornly watching me leave. He'd offered to take the day off and drive me wherever I wanted to go, but I said no. I needed to be on my own.

Driving his Jeep is out of the question as I can't drive a stick shift.

It seems every car on Aegina is a stick shift so I can't rent one. Elena suggested a dune buggy or a scooter.

This is how I ended up on a cute pink scooter, a matching Hello Kitty helmet firmly buckled under my chin.

I have a map of Aegina in my basket and a beach towel strapped to the back. A quick scooter driving lesson and I'm ready to go. Drum roll, please!

I know instinctively what I want to see first without looking at the map.

"Where's the Municipal Theater?" I ask the scooter rental representative.

He points me in the right direction and I follow the small roads through town to the Cathedral of Aegina. The theater, he said, is next to the elaborate red-dome church.

When I arrive in front of an old, faded yellow stone building with peeling paint revealing exposed rock, I sigh. I don't know what I was expecting, but I imagined a more flourishing establishment.

The slanted roof and historic wooden windows and doors give the theater the look of a soldier. As if it has weathered quite a few battles on the island and survived.

After checking to ensure my scooter is parked safely, I venture inside, calling out hello in English and Greek.

I'm greeted with silence.

The configuration of the stage and seats reveal the building's purpose. This is a theater. No doubt. For small intimate productions.

A thrill of excitement races through my spine.

Yes, it's small, and the outside could use a new paint job, but it's a genuine Greek theater. I glance upwards at the wooden beams crisscrossing the ceiling.

An insane out-of-body feeling comes over me.

I'm floating up there looking down at myself standing on the stage in front of a full house of theatergoers, speaking lines from *Antigone* the famous Greek play.

That vision changes to one of me dressed in a funky outfit, singing, "*Mamma Mia, here I go again,*" from the musical *Mamma Mia*, which is set on a Greek island.

I feel a smile stretching across my face. The first in a while that has nothing to do with anyone but myself.

New Rule: Smile for yourself at least once per day.

"Um . . . can I help you?"

I spin around to find a woman in her 20s, standing in front of a side entrance I hadn't noticed.

Denim shorts and a tank top reveal long tanned legs and arms. Her dark hair is tied up in a knot with a wooden pencil sticking out of a makeshift bun.

Her hands and forearms are engulfed in rubber gloves. Dabs of lavender paint dot her face. Her bare feet are splattered with the same paint. She looks like she belongs in a ballgown, not a painting studio.

"You speak English!" My lack of language skills places me at a disadvantage in any foreign country. I've downloaded a language app to rectify that.

The young woman nods, rubbing one of her gloved hands along her neck, and leaving behind a large purple streak on her skin.

"How can I be of help?" she asks formally.

I smile. "I'm here for the summer visiting the Christos Olive Farm."

Before I can finish introducing myself, the woman tilts her head. A slow smile creases her lips. "You must be Bridget."

"You know who I am?"

The woman peels off her gloves and steps forward her hand extended. "I'm Iona Galanis."

My Hello Kitty helmet tumbles out of my arms and lands with a thud on the floor. It spins at my feet before coming to a stop.

"Oh."

Her hand hangs in mid-air. I hurriedly stick out my own hand to shake hers. My tongue sticks to the roof of my mouth.

Suddenly, I'm aware of my helmet head. My curls are smashed down flat on top of my head. Beads of sweat run down my back. Even though she's splattered with paint, she looks way prettier than I ever could.

"Congratulations to you and Ajax," she says, her eyes not meeting mine.

I gulp. Say something, Bridget. Don't just stand here like a robot.

"Thank you?" My voice slides up at the end.

Great! Now she'll think I'm not sure I should be congratulated for snagging the man meant for her.

"I knew Ajax in high school. He's a great guy. But I'm sure you already know that."

I nod numbly.

"How long *have* you known him?"

"Six months . . . ," I stammer out.

Her eyes narrow a teeny bit. It doesn't detract from her goddess-good looks, lavender paint and all.

"Oh," she says. "That's not very long. It must have been love at first sight. I didn't realize Ajax was such a romantic."

I find myself nodding again. I'm a puppet led by a string of lies.

She stands before me all poised and confident while my brain scrambles for something intelligent to add to the conversation.

I look around the room for inspiration. "Do you have any shows scheduled?"

"Aegina's Theater Festival runs from mid-July to mid-August."

I feel my eyes widening. "You have a theater festival on the island?"

She nods. "The island has an awesome artistic presence. Many leading actors and artists summer here or pass through Aegina to perform at the festival."

"Like who?" I ask, fascinated.

"Like Eleni Karakasi, George Kapoutzidis, Elisavet Konstantinidi, Thodoris Atheridis, Smaragda Karydi, Marios Fragkoulis, Christos Mantakas, Antonis Loudaros, Maximos Moumouris, Olia Lazaridou, Giorgos Nanouris, Nadia Kontogiorgi." She ticks off the names on her fingers.

I'm embarrassed I don't recognize any.

"They're pretty well-known here, even if not in the United States."

"I'm sure," I whisper.

We both glance at the stage.

Suddenly, I'm overcome with the feeling that I'm supposed to be here. In Aegina. Standing in this theater.

"Do *you* like the theater, Bridget?" Iona asks slowly.

I nod. My mind is racing. Do I dare say more? What about Ajax? What about me!

I turn my gaze to the beautiful woman whose fiancé I've basically stolen and get ready to beg.

"The truth is, Iona, I love the theater." I squint up my face, forcing the next words to come out of my mouth. "I'm an . . . an actress."

"You are?" Her expressive eyes darken like pools under a midnight sky. "I didn't hear that."

"Well, I am. An actress." I speak much louder than the conversation requires. As if I'm demonstrating I can project my voice to the back of the room and beyond.

"An amateur one," I add. "I've performed in many plays and musicals. Mostly the lead roles."

Okay, hush now Bridget, you sound like you're bragging. I envision myself fist-bumping the air above my head as if I've won a prize. Which is how I feel. I haven't been able to say the words, 'I'm an actress' . . . in . . . *ever*.

Just in case she or anyone in a ten-mile radius didn't already hear me, I repeat loudly. "I'm an actress. I'd love to help in any way I can for the Aegina Theater Festival. I can paint scenery." I indicate her paint-streaked hands and feet. "I can be an understudy or a swing . . . or whatever the acting substitute is called here."

She listens intently. "We could always use more help."

I beam. "What plays are being staged for the festival?"

Iona reaches into her back pocket and whips out a folded piece of paper. She shakes the paper in the air. "I'm afraid it's in Greek."

"It's all Greek to *me*." I laugh and wish I'd kept my mouth shut when I see her frown. She might be one of those literal people who lack a sense of humor.

"I meant the plays are staged in Greek. With English subtitles on a screen." She stares at me. "So . . ."

My shoulders collapse. The excitement drains out of me. "Ah, I get it. I can't be in the plays because I don't speak Greek."

"Right."

"But you can still help if you want to."

"Thanks. I rented a scooter to do some sightseeing on my own for the day. But I'll come back another time."

"Great." She flicks away some paint that's peeling off the wall. "I'm the only one working on the sets during the day. Others will arrive later after their jobs."

This seems like the perfect opening for me to ask what she usually does on Aegina. Like what's her real job.

"You're wondering what I'm doing here, aren't you?"

I smile. "A bit. I don't want to be nosy."

"My grandmother was an actress. She was one of the founders of the Aegina Theater Festival. She passed away two years ago. This year is the first time we're doing it without her."

I blink. "I'm sorry about your grandmother."

"Thanks. Ajax didn't tell us you were an actress."

My heart skips a beat. When did he talk to her about me? And who is "us?" But I don't want to sound paranoid. Although I'm feeling a bit outnumbered.

"I'm just getting back into it." The moment the words come out of my mouth, I feel they are true. I thought I was trying to make conversation, but no. I mean them.

And if I mean them — which I do — then how can I start acting again in a place where all the performances are in a language I don't speak?

I look down at the floor. Another obstacle between me and Ajax.

"It was nice to meet you, Bridget," Iona says, pulling her gloves back on. "I've got to finish before the paint dries. As I said, you can find me here most days. At least until the end of the summer. If you ever have time to help out behind the scenes, we'd be happy to have you."

"Thanks," I murmur. "It was nice meeting you, too." I turn to walk out the front door.

"Tell Ajax I said hello. He's welcome to come help, too."

I don't think she realizes it, but her tone softened when she said that. As if she has feelings for him.

Although she's been speaking in a casual friendly manner the whole time, her parting words stop me in my tracks. I turn back around to see if the expression on her face matches her tone of voice.

Does Iona Galanis have feelings for Ajax? How could she not? He's hot. And kind. And emotionally available.

More importantly, Iona Galanis is no longer a blank face in my mind. She's real. She's beautiful. She seems kind. She loves the arts, which is a huge plus in my books. She's also available.

"Bridget Walker!" my inner voice screams, "They speak the same language, they live in the same place, and . . . she loves olives and farming."

What the heck am I doing getting in Fate's way?

Chapter Thirty-Two

BRIDGET

The benefit of being in a fake relationship is that jealousy is irrelevant. How can I be jealous of another woman liking my fake man? I can't. Which makes the blood roiling through my veins at the idea of them together also irrelevant. Right?

I jam the Hello Kitty helmet on my head and push my scooter off the sidewalk. I forget about maps, ancient sites, and photo ops.

I ride along the curving coastline, trying to forget about Ajax and Iona, and really anything to do with relationships.

I want to be a carefree woman on vacation where the only thing on my mind is the warm island breeze ruffling the curls on my shoulders.

I stop to tie one of Ajax's bandanas around my neck. To be an island girl. When I inhale his woodsy scent still clinging to the fabric, I yank it off and throw it into my backpack.

What is wrong with you? I snap. A piece of cloth is making you miss him? For real?

I start back up on the scooter determined to make the most of my day alone.

I rumble along paved and dirt roads. Past churches and chapels of all shapes and sizes. The pristine blue sea beckons to me to take a dip.

I end up in a small seaside village. A fleet of white fishing boats bob in the cutest curved harbor, their decks covered with bright piles of nets and buoys.

Bougainvillea flowers in a startling fuchsia and the palest of pinks hang over walls, dripping their petals onto the concrete.

I'm from Maine. We've got a lot of harbors. None as adorable as this.

A concrete promenade curves alongside the bay. Small shops selling everything from fishing rods and nets to phone cards and sexy beach cover-ups, invite me to step inside and purchase souvenirs for my sisters.

Neat blue and white tavernas dot the sea wall. The scent of meats roasting on charcoals invades my senses. I didn't even realize I was hungry until I hear my stomach make horrible grumbling noises.

It's all so picture-perfect. I'm surprised it's not swarming with tourists. I head for the nearest empty table and chair.

A vision stops me in my tracks.

I could live here. I could be a part of this life every day. Ride a scooter around Aegina. Stop here whenever I want. Eat amazing Greek food. Join the theater, somehow. If only I was Ajax's . . . the vision stops abruptly in my head. Ajax's what?

My phone rings in my bag. I dig it out and Ajax's face appears, a frown marring his smooth skin.

"What's wrong?" I ask instantly.

The frown disappears. "Bridget!"

"Ajax!" I match his enthusiasm.

"I was worried about you. I tried calling a few times, but you didn't answer."

"I was riding. I didn't hear it. Or maybe I was out of a service area."

He's staring at something over my shoulder. "Are you in Vathi?"

I glance around for a sign of where I've landed. I shrug. "I don't know. I just followed my nose."

He laughs. "All of the restaurants there are good. How was your day so far? I miss you."

"I miss you, too." It slips out.

His smile is worth the slip.

"What have you seen?"

I start to tell him about meeting Iona, but stop myself. I'd rather tell him in person. The fact that I'm going to wait is so unlike me. I always want to dive into anything as soon as it happens. But talking about his arranged marriage needs our full attention. Especially if I want to find out how he really feels.

"I'll tell you everything later when I get back home."

The look of happiness on his face has me asking, "Why the big cheesy grin?"

"You said, 'back home.' Meaning Christos Farms is . . ."

I nod swiftly. "I get it. While I'm in Aegina."

He doesn't stop smiling. "I'm glad you feel that way."

"I was just thinking about how my life would be if I lived here."

I swear his eyes are going to fall out. "Really?"

"Yes, it's a beautiful island. And . . . well, never mind."

"You can tell me about it when you get home, okay?"

I nod my head. Looking at him through the phone, I'm reminded of how incomplete I felt talking to him from thousands of miles away.

Today, I'll see him later in person. We'll share a meal, tell each other stories of our day, while sitting side by side. Maybe I'll kiss him again, who knows?

I hang up with mixed feelings. I'm excited to see him later. But

I'm sad too. Knowing it'll be back to phone calls and video chats before we know it.

I pick one of the tavernas and order by pointing to pictures on the menu since it's in Greek. The meal I'm presented looks like it could be for an entire family. No way I can eat all of this.

I thank the server who keeps coming with dish after dish. Piles of scorching hot chicken and lamb skewers. Crispy fries, platters of prawns, calamari, and bowls of salad and hummus with puffed pita.

A striped kitten weaves its way between my legs, begging for a bit of my lunch. I slip him a fry. He reminds me of Freckles. I never thought I'd miss that cat, but I do.

If I lived in Aegina, I would get a cat. Ajax has his dog Zorro, who is too old to do much anymore. I'd introduce a kitten into our lives.

Whoa! What am I thinking?

The waiter returns to offer me a carafe of wine. I point to my pink scooter sitting under a branch of pink flowers. "No thanks, I'm driving."

He grins, returning with a fruity drink that tastes like pomegranates. When I ask, he tells me it *is* pomegranates and that the fruit grows all over the island.

"Of course, they do," I say, before taking another big sip of nectar from the gods.

How can one place contain all my favorite things?

I savor my meal, staring out at the sparkling sea, wondering where the giant ferries chugging by in the distance are headed.

The sunshine, the food, the beach, and the pomegranate drink work together to lull me into a sense of profound peace. Like the peace I felt with Ajax when I kissed him.

With so many new experiences and feelings, I'm glad I got alone time to process them.

After my lavish meal, I spread a towel on one of the flat rocks and dangle my feet over the sea. Before long, I lay down and doze off, sheltered by Ajax's bandana on my face.

My ringing phone interrupts my afternoon seaside nap.

"This better be good," I answer.

"It is good!" Daisy's voice exclaims.

I pop up into a seated position, tucking my legs under me. "Daisy," I cry. "I miss you so much."

"Yeah, sure you do. That's why you call me so often." She pouts over the video call.

Before I can say a word, she shouts, "Is that a beach? Are you at the beach?"

I turn the phone around for her to see the beautiful fishing village.

"I'm so jealous."

"I hope you will come see it one day."

"Like when you and Ajax get married?"

"Hush. We're not getting married."

"Sure, you're not."

"Seriously, Daisy. I met the woman he's supposed to marry today. Iona Galanis. She's perfect for him. In every way."

"Except he doesn't want her. He wants *you*."

"I don't know about that," I mumble.

Daisy sighs. "What'd you do?"

"He told me he loves me. I didn't say it back."

"He told you he loved you?" Daisy screams. "That's so . . . oh, Bridget I can't wait to hear those words from a guy. What did you say back?"

"I said I loved him, but not as a boyfriend."

Daisy makes her judgy *tssk tssk* noises. "What else?"

"I told him he lives here, and I live there, so . . ."

Daisy's head drops into her hand. "You played the long-distance card."

"It's not a card. It's the truth."

"It's an excuse." She raises her head and scowls at me. "You always do that, you know. You run away as soon as anyone says they like you for more than a friend."

"How do you know that?" I ask, although she's right.

"Um . . . every single boy you've ever dated has complained to Ava, and Corrine and I heard them talking."

"Oh!"

"I understand you're scared."

"I'm not scared." How dare my baby sister who is only eighteen and never been kissed tell me I'm scared. "You don't know anything."

She purses her lips at me. "Really? You want to go there?"

"No. I was feeling so nice and peaceful before you called."

She grins. "Sorry to mess up your *peaceful* vibe. But Bridget, you love Ajax. We can all see it. Even Daddy."

"It doesn't matter if I love him. We can't be together forever."

"Why are you so sure you can't be with him forever?"

I don't know if it's the heat, the fact that I've been alone all day, or that I miss Ajax after just a few hours apart, but I sob out, "Because one day he'll *die*."

I drop the phone. Bury my head in my hands. Loud sobs rip through me.

I blow my nose on Ajax's bandana and try to wipe my tears away. When I close my eyes, all I can see is me standing next to a gravesite.

Finally, I pick up the phone to see Daisy wiping tears from her own eyes.

"I'm sorry." I touch the screen where her lovely face is so far away from me. "I didn't mean to make you cry too."

"We all miss her, Bridget. I was only seven when she died, I miss her all the time. It's okay to miss her. It's okay to be sad."

"I should be comforting you. I'm the bigger sister."

"We can comfort each other. That's what Mom would want."

I feel as if I've been physically stabbed. The pain is visceral and real. I look down and expect to see blood on my hands.

"Is that why you won't allow yourself to fall in love with Ajax? Because you're worried about losing him like Mom?"

"Maybe," I gulp.

Daisy clasps her hands together as if she's praying. Maybe she is. We look at each other in silence. I see from her eyes that my baby sister is stronger, braver than me.

"Wouldn't you rather love him for as long as you can, than never love him at all?" she asks.

I shake my head back and forth. "I can't handle the pain of it. If I lose him. I wouldn't be able to handle it."

Daisy's eyes brim with sadness and pity for me. I wrap my arms around myself.

"You're strong, Bridget," she says. "You must trust yourself."

I shake my head again. "You must know yourself before you can trust yourself. And I'm sorry, Daisy, but I don't think I know myself."

Even as the last words leave my lips, I know they're not completely true. I do know myself a little. I know I love my family. I know I feel my best on a stage. And I know without a doubt, that I love Ajax Christos.

Which is why I decide that I won't be telling him I met the woman he's *supposed* to marry. I'm not ready to lose him as yet.

Chapter Thirty-Three

AJAX

Bridget's voice filters through the trees while she works on the patio. Since she returned from her lone adventure, she's been pulling all nighters working on her projects.

I fixed up an old scooter we had in the garage and sprayed it pink for her so she can have her own transportation now. The light in her eyes when I presented it to her took my breath away.

"It's nothing," I said. "I just put air in the tires and got it tuned up. I think every Aegina family has one of these old scooters sitting around."

She threw her arms around my neck. "I love it."

"Well, it's all yours."

Sometimes, she disappears during the day, not telling me where she's going, saying it's a surprise. I see her zooming down the driveway and my heart hitches. In a good way, because it means she's making her own life on Aegina.

But also, in a slightly nervous way. Because she's not sharing it with me, and we always shared everything before.

Like how she happily includes me in video chats with her family to share their joy about the upcoming opening of Ava's Gelateria.

Or their drama over Daisy and Emerald's love triangle with Jackson. I make sure and put on a shirt before getting in front of the camera.

I'll never live down the time I didn't, and they heckled me, calling me Magic Mike and begging me to dance with the patio chair.

So embarrassing!

But I've come to feel like a part of Bridget's family as much as she's becoming a part of mine. At least I hope so.

This is why the week leading up to the engagement/marketing plan party is probably the best week of my life — well, other than the week Elena was born when I was fourteen years old and I got to carry her around like a doll in a blanket.

I wake up earlier than usual to do my part of the farm work and then spend the entire day with Bridget, driving around the island for her to do more photo shoots with my family and friends.

The official theme of our party and the Olive oil campaign is "*Arete.*" It's a Greek word that means virtue or excellence, but it also translates to being your highest self.

So, Bridget has adopted that Greek word and made it our new company logo.

Arete, Being our Best Self.

It's ironic because, with her, I do feel like I'm being my highest self. I'm happy all the time. Except when I think about her leaving at the end of the summer.

And I have a clear vision, for the future of the farm even if not for our relationship.

Living with Arete means you'll flourish, and that's what I plan on doing. If Bridget's plans are not in sync with mine, I'll adapt and adjust as we go along.

The same way I do with growing the best olives possible. As far as I can tell, watching Papa and Mama grow their relationship is very much like growing an olive tree. Maybe easier.

I chuckle out loud and Bridget looks up from her phone where she's writing notes from our last stop at Tia Ziona and Tio Sebastian's home. She smiles at me and goes back to her note-taking.

The more family we visit, the more Bridget is welcomed. I'm not surprised that everyone wants to meet her. She's hugged and fed, patted and kissed by the oldest to the youngest of my family members.

They're all, "Come in Bridget. You're a beautiful girl, Bridget. Sit down, and have a cup of coffee, Bridget. Ajax, go outside to the chiller and get some cheese to go with Bridget's raisin bread, or rustic bread, or sesame bread."

Then Bridget is all, "Thank you. It's so great to meet you. Oh, this is delicious. Did you make it yourself?" which she's realized is a question that will bring frowns.

Of course they did, who else would make it? Then Bridget would exclaim and they would offer her the recipe or invite her to come by one morning and bake with them.

This would be followed by an hour of conversation where they all speak excitedly, as I sit back and watch.

She's the extrovert to my quiet, farmer personality.

Inside my head is a whole world of dialogue that emerges only with her. With my best friend Tyler, I talk a lot about life and work. With Bridget, I can discuss those topics, but also everything else in the world.

"You're awfully quiet," Bridget says shutting her phone down and leaning back with a sigh in the passenger seat.

We drive along the hills, slowing down as we enter the small traditional village of Perdika, with its wharves jutting into the protected cove. Tied-up fishing boats bob in the clear waters after returning with their fresh catch of the day.

Perdika's secret is how it manages to stay low-key while featuring red-tiled roof boutique hotels and a shaded balcony promenade that houses shops and restaurants serving the fresh catch of the day. Christos Olive Oil is sold in the souvenir shops and served in many of the restaurants.

The best part is the little ferry that carries passengers back and forth to an offshore island for a day of beaches, goats, and good food.

"Can we have another beach day soon?" Bridget stares out the window at beautiful Perdika. The sea is a shimmering expanse of blues and greens. It's a perfect summer day.

My heart pings.

"Of course, we can. What about today?"

"I didn't bring my swimsuit. Or a towel, or anything really." Her face clouds with disappointment. "I need to remember we live on this gorgeous island and should always be prepared."

Did she just say "*we?*" My heart does more than ping. It kicks up its heels.

I quickly debate whether to swing the Jeep around and race home for her to pick up her swimsuit. Or stop at one of the shops in the village to buy her one right now. Why waste time?

Arete, remember. Be in the moment and live it the best I know how.

I turn the steering wheel hard. We zip up a side road that most people don't know about. It traverses a field of lemon trees.

She does a yoga inhale from her seat. "This air is incredible."

"Lemons," I say and point out my window.

She shakes her head. "Is there anything Aegina doesn't have? Pistachios, olives, pomegranates, and now, lemons!"

"And me." I say it boldly, but my heart is holding its breath.

"Especially you." She gifts me the sweetest smile and I swear I feel like a teenager falling in love with a movie star.

I park the Jeep happier than I've ever been! So what if I get a bit ahead of myself. I am in love with this woman. Even if I can't tell her that again.

I want her to be my fiancée for real. Even if I can't tell her that *ever*!

I wonder if my forebears who created philosophy and the whole Arete lifestyle would have some advice to share with me now?

"Where're we going?" Bridget stands in the middle of the tiny road, bag under her arm and phone in her hand. She's pointing her camera at everything she sees.

"Shopping."

"For real?"

"Yes, my dear."

"You're joking."

"I am not."

"For what though? We have almost everything we need for the party, and for the olive oil launch."

I take her hand as we stroll along the shady sidewalk, the leaves of eucalyptus trees breaking up the hot sunshine.

"I would like to buy you a gift."

She drops my hand. "I don't need a gift. I'm happy doing everything I'm doing."

I smile to reassure her. "It's a gift so we can go straight to the beach. Or rather to that island over there. I point to Moni in the near distance."

Her eyes gleam. "We're going to another island? You're taking me shopping for a swimsuit?"

You'd think I was taking her to buy a royal cloak and tiara. "Yes."

She rubs her hands together in glee. "This is going to be awesome."

"I hope so."

I can't wait to float in the water with her again. Or just lay in one of the hammocks together on the idyllic island.

Chapter Thirty-Four

AJAX

An hour later, more or less, we're doing exactly that. Bridget found what she describes as the supreme two-piece swimsuit that has ties everywhere — around her neck, across her creamy dark hips, and in front of her breasts.

I do my best not to be "that" guy and ogle my fake fiancée.

"You can look, dude," she teases me, when I cover my eyes with one hand as she exits the fitting room and spins in front of me.

"I've never seen so much of you before."

"Pssst, yes you have."

"On video chat while you sit on your bed in a tank top and panties eating cookies doesn't count."

She giggles. "Shhhh!" She glances around the small swim store. Two of the young assistants were in lower grades than me in high school. They're blushing and smiling at me now.

"You're like a superstar here, aren't you?" Bridget teases again.

I shrug. "Not really."

But there's no doubting the amount of attention thrown my way as Bridget and I make our way through the village.

Friends from bars and tavernas hail us and call me inside for a quick drink. I deflect them all and say we're headed for a swim.

"Maybe later," Bridget hoots.

"If we stop to drink at every bar and restaurant you promised to return to, we'll be intoxicated for the rest of the week."

She smashes that thought with a flick of her wrist. "Live a little. This is so much fun! After our big event this weekend, we're hanging out in this village. I think it may be my favorite so far. I want to try these Greek fish dishes. Maybe even eat octopus."

I beam at her. "Sounding like a local."

"I'm down for hanging out after our party," I agree.

I can play the social game with the best of them, but do I like to? Not really. I was not the party guy at Harvard. A couple of close friends, some wine, discussing world events. That was more my scene.

I already know Bridget was the party girl back in high school and college. And until lately, she was at the center of Boston's singles scene.

I can't compete with the excitement of a club scene, the DJs, and dancing. But I hope she likes me for me and trust in that.

We leap onto the ferry without a moment to spare.

The captain is an old school buddy so he held it when I called ahead to say we were coming.

Bridget slides into an open seat and I stand between her legs, balancing with a wide-legged stance and one hand on the ceiling.

"This is gorgeous," Bridget says, spinning around to watch us depart from the mainland. I almost feel like singing one of the *Mamma Mia* songs."

"Go right ahead," I tease.

Her eyes twinkle. "You dare me?"

I blink. God, I love this woman.

"Dare."

"How much?"

I pull out a five-euro bill and slap it down on the bench. She grabs it before it flies away in the breeze.

"I was thinking a kiss," she says slyly. "If I sing, you can kiss me. If I don't, I'll keep your money."

"Wait, so you win either way?" I shake my head. "Fine. Please sing."

I really think she's kidding. And that I've lost my five bucks. But no.

Bridget stands up and grabs the metal pole in the middle of the ferry. She smiles at the passengers. "If you know the words, please join in."

The ferry is small but it's full of people from all over the world — Germans, Swedes, Chinese, East Indians, and some Aussies, based on their down-under accents.

She scrolls on her phone. The next thing I know, one of ABBA's most famous songs, *Dancing Queen* is playing.

Bridget sings along, her lovely, melodious voice rising above the sound of the engine.

I don't know about the other passengers, but I'm mesmerized.

The captain raises a thumbs up at me and I can't help the silly grin on my face. Is she amazing or what?

The ferry nears the tiny island of Moni. Pine trees wave in the breeze from the island surrounded by a sea that looks like a blanket of diamonds.

Bridget's voice soars. I've heard her sing karaoke in Italy, so I know her voice is incredible, but she sounds even better outdoors surrounded by the elements.

The passengers can't help themselves. Every single person joins her in singing *Dancing Queen*. By the time we dock, the folks who are already sunning themselves on the island have stood up.

They clap and cheer as our captain ties up the ferry.

Bridget leaps out the side of the boat with my helping hand and takes a bow.

Her curls are a wild halo around her face. Her skin is burnished from the sun. Her sexy black swimsuit fits perfectly.

"Want that kiss now?" she whispers in my ear.

Every nerve ending in my body is on high alert to her soft voice in my ear. "Oh yes, madam. Let me get you out of the spotlight first."

She laughs. "Dude, I live for the spotlight."

THE SUN IS SETTING AFTER HOURS OF SWIMMING, lounging on the beach, drinking wine from a bottle, and eating souvlakis wrapped in wax paper. Bridget makes a mess dropping sauce and wine all over her lap. Good thing there's the warm sea right here to rinse off in.

She grabs my hand and makes me jump into the sea with her.

All my worries about her leaving at the end of summer, the olive harvest being a success, the bills piling up, vanish as soon as she kisses me.

And boy does she kiss me.

I sink down as far as I can go. My feet smack the bottom and I spring back up like a jet. The entire world changes.

I have no idea how my life got so amazing, but I'm thanking all the Greek gods and goddesses for leading me to Italy last year. And bringing her here to me.

Bridget treads water close to me and wraps her arms around my neck. "I want another kiss."

"Demanding."

"Absolutely." She plants kisses along my collarbone, and I shiver in the hot sun.

I wrap my arms around her and pull her close. She wraps her legs around my waist and a rush of sparks ignite my entire body.

I wipe everything else out of my mind. I don't know how long our kiss lasts as the sea circles us in gentle waves.

"We should kiss more often," she says, squeezing water from her hair onto my shoulders with a devilish smile.

"I agree. I don't know why it took you so long to get with the program."

She pushes at my shoulders and breaks away from my hold, laughing happily.

"My sisters would love it here," Bridget says gazing around at the sea, sky, rocks, and Aegina nearby.

I gather her body close to me again. "We can invite them all. Any time you want."

"Maybe for the olive harvest. We can come to shake down the trees. I would like to experience that."

She knows harvest is in October or early November, so what is she implying? Is she saying she'll come back two months after she leaves? If she leaves? Why leave?

Don't think of the future Ajax, I warn myself. But how can I not? My entire existence is based on forecasting the future . . . weather patterns, climate, olive yield . . . and now a future love.

"You're so serious. What are you thinking about?"

"About you never leaving me." That's what I want to say. I don't.

I let go of her and duck under the sea. Bubbles escape my mouth and I clamp my lips shut. I come up spitting water.

Bridget leaps onto my back, clinging like a monkey and I spin her around. I kiss her glistening brown arms wrapped around my neck. "You need to wear more sunblock, missy. Look at your skin peeling."

"And you need to stop making me dizzy."

I don't want Bridget to know my secret wish of her staying in Aegina, making a life here with me and my entire family. If she does, she'll stop kissing and start retreating.

I've waited this long for a girlfriend. She's a gift from the Greek gods themselves. It's a travesty to throw away a gift from the universe.

Arete!

Chapter Thirty-Five

BRIDGET

The night before the fake engagement/reveal party, I plan a video call with my family and invite Ajax to join me.

My days have been filled with preparing for the party, finalizing the rebranding presentation, and helping with the theater festival in town.

The theater is my little secret. I'm painting sets and helping the stage manager. They love my ideas. I feel as if I'm tip-toeing back to the place I love most of all. I'm just not ready to share it with anyone.

Plus, there's Iona Galanis. She's nice but I have a funny feeling she's biding her time. Waiting for me to leave town. Which is why I haven't told Ajax we're working together.

My evenings are all about him.

We met up with his friends at their favorite bar in town since our trip to Moni. We decided it would be best if I met them before the party.

During dart games, glasses of beer and wine, and a lot of laughing, I discovered there's no bowling alley on Aegina.

"So, what's the bowling team?" I asked Ajax.

Between fits of laughter, Alicia, one of Ajax's best friends, admitted that the 'Bowling Team' was what they called themselves when they were in middle school.

"But why?" I asked.

"He started it," she pointed at Ajax. "He always said, 'Shut up and bowl,' to get us to do something."

I smiled to think of Ajax as a bossy pre-teen. "So, it stuck huh."

"We got bowling shirts with the saying on the back. He still says it to us."

"Shut up and bowl, Alicia," Ajax laughed, handing her the darts for her turn.

"That's like me and my sisters. We say, 'Go get the muffins.' When we're trying to get one of them to leave the room."

Everyone laughed with me.

"You guys are a perfect couple," Alicia said. "Rude and bossy."

Ajax slid an arm around my waist. I leaned into him. "We try," I said.

No one blinked an eye when he kissed the tip of my nose. Least of all me.

"Finally!" I shout when I see my entire family in front of the screen. It's very late my time, but that's okay because I'm too excited to be tired.

Ava and Tyler are sitting on a stool around the kitchen counter. Daisy and Emerald are on the other side of the center island. Corrine is fiddling with the volume on the iPad.

Dad and Maxine are leaning against the side counter. Dad has his arms around Maxine, and they look like a mom and dad. My stomach clenches missing the woman who would have been standing next to Dad.

"Bridget!" they all shout at me.

Tears prick the backs of my eyelids. Seeing them all together, smiling and looking darker brown from the summer sun. I just want to hug them all.

I introduce Ajax to Maxine who is the only one who hasn't met him through a video call before.

Tyler waves at Ajax and Ajax waves back, calling out, "What's up man?"

The two guys share a few bits of news about their college friends while my family and I listen and wink or stick our tongues out at each other with undisguised joy.

"Who's got news?" I ask. "I want all the latest."

Emerald waves her hand in the air. "Me!"

"Wait," Dad says, pulling down Emmie's arm. "Let's hear what Ajax and Bridget have been up to. How's the rebranding going of your family's olive oil?" Dad speaks to Ajax.

Ajax shrugs. "Bridget's keeping it a big secret. All I know is that she's designed a campaign around the Greek word, 'Arete,' which means being your best.

"And she's unveiling her promotions and advertising ideas for the entire line of products tomorrow at our party. In front of our entire family."

"Wow!" Dad says, and it's echoed by all my sisters. "You're having a party to celebrate the rebranding? That's exciting."

Ajax and I exchange looks. I'd told him I wanted to share the secret with my family, but he said if I told them about the fake engagement, we had to tell his family. So, for now, our fake engagement is still hush hush.

"The ideas flowed as soon as I got here, met the extended family, and of course, tried the olive oil." This part is all true.

"That's great, Bridget," Dad says. "We're proud of you. Have you fallen in love with Aegina?"

"Yes," I say, catching Ajax's dark eyes. "The island is amazing. You'll have to come here one day, preferably during the olive harvest so we can all shake down the trees together. That's how they do it."

My sisters blink in unison. No one says a word.

"Hold up," Corrine leans into the screen. "What have you done with our Bridget who loves the glamorous life?"

I shrug. Ajax laughs. "This is Bridget 2.0. She lives in flip-flops and rubber boots now."

"I really love the trees. They're like family members."

"I bet that's what she loves," Daisy mumbles.

Tyler barks out a laugh. So does Corrine.

Ajax is oblivious. His eyes are shooting beams of adoration at me. Dad and my sisters are not going to miss what is becoming clear. Ajax likes me a lot more than a best friend.

We're kissing, holding hands, and snuggling to watch Netflix movies late at night. Like a real couple.

He may have accidentally blurted out that he loved me. But he hasn't mentioned it since. We don't talk about us. It's a taboo subject. As far as I know, he's okay with me leaving at the end of summer. And what's happening is a summer fling. Nothing more, nothing less.

"I'll be sad when I have to leave Aegina," I say solemnly. I'm looking at my family but I'm speaking to Ajax. I hope he realizes this.

"So, tell me your news. I want to know everything," I abruptly change the subject to get away from the disaster of me and Ajax having to say goodbye.

All hell breaks loose as Emerald, Daisy, and Corrine all try to talk at once.

I turn to Corrine. "Hey sis, what's the big announcement you mentioned in your text?"

Corrine sits up straighter. Her lips tilt in a small smile. "I'm going to do my senior year of college abroad."

"What!" I leap up from the sofa. "Where?"

"Portugal. You know that's one of the languages I've studied for my major. I get to go for an entire year to teach English and finish up there."

"OMG!" I squeal. "That's fantastic!"

"She got a fellowship," Dad says from the back. "We are so proud of our girl."

I clap my hands. "Congratulations, sis. You'll love traveling abroad." I glance down at Ajax on the sofa and sit back next to him. "It'll change your life for sure."

"When do you leave for Portugal?" Ajax asks.

Corrine glances at her phone. "In a couple of weeks. I'm going to settle into my housing and get the lay of the land, so to speak."

"Ohhh!" I squeal. "I'll still be here." I look at Ajax. He looks at me. At the same time, we both say, "Come here!"

There's a lot of squealing and clapping and nodding on my family's side. "I can do that," Corrine says. "My ticket gets me to Lisbon. Once I settle my stuff in my new home, which is in Porto, I can hop over on one of those cheap airlines around Europe."

I look over at Ajax. "Is that okay are you sure she can come?" I say it all in a rush of breath.

He nods hard. "I would love to meet you, Corrine."

"It's settled then," Dad says looking sad. "I've lost two daughters to the dark side."

"Oh, hush Daddy," Daisy says patting his hand. "You have us. Plus, Maxine. And Freckles." She waves one of Freckles' paws at me.

Elena comes up behind me and wraps her skinny arms around my neck from behind. "Is this them?" she squeals.

"Why are you out of bed?" Ajax demands.

"I heard a lot of noise," Elena pouts. "Can I meet them?"

A chorus of "Hi, Elena," sing songs through the iPad. Elena comes around and sits on the floor in front of me and Ajax, face level with the screen.

"Hello, everybody. Can I guess who you are?"

My sisters laugh. "Yes, who am I?" Corrine asks.

Elena tilts her head. She points at Emerald and guesses right. "You are the baby of the family. I can tell because you're in the middle of everyone."

Emerald laughs. "I'll always be the baby."

Elena agrees. "Me, too. Right, Ajax?"

He ruffles her hair. "Yes."

Next Elena picks out Daisy. "I know you because you're wearing that pink top with ruffles. Bridget says your motto is 'Pink or die.'"

We all giggle. "I like pink, too," Elena says waving one of her pink socked feet in the air from her seated position.

More laughter.

Elena points at Ava. "You're the big sister who loves gelato."

Ava raises a hand and grins. "That's me. My gelato shop opens in a month. I hope you can visit us one day and try it out."

I squeal, "Ava, I'm so proud of you!"

"You'll be back for the grand opening right?" Ava asks.

My heart drops two notches to my stomach. I feel so conflicted about leaving Aegina. Not just because of Ajax, who I can't imagine not seeing every day, but I'm feeling a greater sense of accomplishment here than ever before.

I have free rein to create an international brand.

I have the Municipal Theater. I can't be on stage but I'm painting sets and assisting the stage manager.

Being a part of the Theater Festival is like a dream come true, even if I must hide my connection to Iona Galanis for now.

When the first play opens, I will take Ajax to see it. Once I see them interacting, I will know what to do. I'll know whether to step aside. Or whether to fight for Ajax.

For now, I say, "Sure, Ava. I wouldn't miss it."

"Okay," Elena puts her hand under her chin. "I'm not finished."

She points to Corrine's face and says, "And you are the middle sister. The best things are in the middle. Like the sticky part of a cinnamon roll."

Corrine cracks up. "You're right, Elena. The middle is best."

"Now that I've met you all on the phone, I can't wait to see you in person at the wedding."

Dead silence.

Then a cacophony of voices yell, "What wedding? Whose wedding?"

I cover my mouth with one hand. How could I let it slip out this way?

"Elena, say goodnight, It's time for bed." Ajax ushers his sister out the room. But not before she gives us a side eye that could stop a criminal.

"Later," Ajax mouths to her.

Elena puts two fingers to her eyes, then points them at us in the classic sign of "I'm watching you."

Meanwhile, on the video chat, my family is staring with grim faces.

"Spill it, Bridget," Ava demands.

I have no choice. We tell them the truth. About the arranged marriage right up to the fake engagement party.

By the time I'm done, Daisy is howling with laughter. Dad is sagging against the counter. My other sisters are looking skeptical (Corrine) and mad (Emerald). Ava says she's not judging.

"You both know that lies never win." She dares to glance at Tyler, the man she almost lost because of a lie she told her semester in Italy while studying to be a Gelato Master.

"Trust me, we're trying to save Ajax. It's for a good cause."

Ava nods. "As long as no one is getting hurt."

Dad shakes his head. "Ajax, I don't know how it feels to be in your position with parents trying to arrange a marriage for you. Marriage is the most important step in anyone's life. But I urge you to tell them the truth soon. They deserve to know Bridget is just a friend."

"Yes, sir," Ajax says. "I'll be honest. Bridget is more than just a friend to me."

All eyes swing to the man sitting next to me. Especially my eyes. "What are you saying?"

"Just tell her, dude," Tyler shouts to his best friend. "It's not as if we can't see for ourselves."

Ajax turns to me. He takes one of my hands in his. Looks at me with those deep dark eyes that I can't help but sink into.

The feel of his callused hand rubbing over my knuckles gives me the shivers.

And my Dad is watching!

"Bridget Walker. I love you. I have ever since I first met you and you bossed me around. And I love you more each day we spend together. But I don't know how we can make our lives work together." His voice drops to a whisper. "But I pray we can figure it out."

When he's finished with his declaration, my nosy, loud, pushy, and demanding family clap as one.

Dad wipes one of his eyes. Maxine rubs his back.

Tyler and Ava hug.

Daisy says, "I knew it." She fist pumps the air.

Every single person turns their attention to me.

Ajax's eyes haven't left my face once. I lower my eyes so he can't see the roller coaster of emotions I'm experiencing reflected in them.

They're all waiting for me to say something in response to Ajax's true love speech. I bow my head until I'm eyeballing my belly button.

This is too much pressure. For the one least likely to settle down. The one whose first rule of thumb is don't get attached.

But it seems that Ajax has crossed over from fake to faithful. How do I reel it back to the safety zone?

"I don't know what I feel," I wail. "Please don't make me say anything more." I leap up and race down the hall to my bedroom.

My room is a cool dark haven. I drop down on the bed and cover my head with a pillow.

I forgot my phone in Ajax's room. I wonder what my family thinks of their carefree, don't-get-involved Bridget now?

I wonder what Mom would think? I close my eyes and try to picture her face. Her curly hair, like mine. The way she sat on the arm of the sofa reading lines with me.

She loved to get into character herself, sometimes surprising me with a prop or a funny costume. Like the time she walked into my bedroom sporting a tall striped hat to get in character for practicing my lines for the 8th grade *Cat in the Hat* musical.

She had ordered it online. "Anything worth doing is worth doing well," she told me.

Which is why I know that Mom would want me to be all in. With whatever I choose to do. Not live with one foot in and one foot out, ready to escape when things get dicey. Or when I could lose.

"You won't always get the part, Bridget, but you can always have the satisfaction of trying your best."

Am I trying my best now?

And what about Ajax? Why is it so hard to say those three words to him?

You know why, I cry to myself.

How can I love him and leave him?

How could Mom love me and leave me?

Chapter Thirty-Six

AJAX

The morning of the party I'm up and outside before the sun comes up. I pour out a mug of hot coffee and stroll through the olive pathways, touching my beloved tree trunks, feeling their solidness, their roots to the island my family has lived on for generations.

I am these trees, and they are me. I know I can't leave here. But what about losing Bridget? Can I live here happily without her?

The phone call with Bridget's family messed with my head in many ways.

It's clear that although Bridget may love the island and my family, she's not certain about her feelings for me.

And more importantly, she is returning home. Even if she talks about being on the island, her mind is set that we belong to our own worlds. Hers to her family in Maine, and me to mine here.

How could I possibly be upset about it? I understand her reasons very well. I have to prepare my heart for her leaving me. If I don't, I'll be blindsided by it. Like not protecting a tree from frost or insects when you know it's coming.

I would be a neglectful farmer if I ignored something so important, knowing danger is brewing.

Which puts us where exactly with this engagement party today?

I glance at my watch. In eight hours, all the tents will be up, the screen to reveal the newly rebranded olive oil will be unfolded, and the food and wine will be served to my family and friends.

I need to get through today. Enjoy the moments, and cherish them. Try not to let my thoughts bounce around like a ping pong ball.

Chapter Thirty-Seven

BRIDGET

I wake up just as the sun is shining through the slats of the big picture window that faces the olive forest. As soon as I remember how I ran out on Ajax last night, a sinking feeling invades my heart.

He's been nothing but wonderful to me!

I could have said, "I love you too." I could have tried.

I grab my journal and close my eyes. Every day I take the time to write three things I am grateful for. A practice I started when a school counselor advised me to try it years ago.

Today, I write quickly.

I am grateful for my family. I am grateful to be able to use my marketing skills to help the Christos family. My pen hesitates above the paper for the last thing I am grateful for.

I want to write Ajax and our growing closeness. It's something I have written before, something I am grateful for. But today, my hand is frozen.

I tap my pen against the page. I close my eyes, open them wide, and write, I am grateful to be in Aegina for this beautiful summer abroad.

There, that is what I am grateful for. Ajax is part of all that. It encompasses him without it being all about him.

Aren't we allowed to put boundaries and limits on what we're grateful for?

Never mind, there's too much to do today to dwell on that.

I'm planning on showering and dressing for the party later after all the setting up is done. I hurry down to the kitchen, grab my mug of coffee, and head to the patio.

Elena is already hanging up decorations with her mother. Ajax and Christos are nowhere around.

"Big day," Mrs. Christos smiles at me.

I nod nervously. This is much more than a fake engagement party.

It's my chance to show the Christos family my plans that could increase their sales tremendously. If they love it. If they agree to showcase their lives and give up some of their peace and serenity for some good old TikTok videos I expect may go viral when people see this gorgeous island, its food, and of course, the farm-to-table olive oil.

I haven't even touched the tip of what this island offers in my presentation. I will have to teach someone about shooting great videos to keep the content fresh. I will need to supervise from afar, which will make this harder, but we can do it.

When Ajax and his father return from taking care of the trees, we all pitch in to erect the tents and set up the long tables and chairs that were delivered early this morning.

I step backward and take it all in.

We're using one side of the tent flap as a screen to showcase the presentation I've put together.

Food is arriving as family members drop them off one by one to return later for the festivities.

The goat is roasting on a spit, which I guess was set up while I was still asleep.

Bowls of food are placed in the chiller outside. I decorate the tables with fragrant olive branches I picked yesterday.

Bowls of fruit sit in the center — ruby red pomegranates, bright yellow lemons, and oranges that look like competition tennis balls.

Jars of wildflowers fill the tables giving them all a festive, fun aura.

It's all so low cost and low key, but elegant in its simplicity.

Mrs. Christos brings out platters of mini cakes. Elena arranges them in cake towers and decorates the base with natural objects like pinecones, leaves, and pebbles. It looks like something out of a country living magazine.

"That's gorgeous, Elena," I tell her.

"Yup," she says a bit coolly. We haven't spoken about the phone call last night. I hang my head. This is what it feels like to be rebuked by a 12-year-old who knows better than I do.

Mrs. Christos wraps an arm around my shoulders. "Don't be sad, Bridget. It's your day."

I feel my lips tilting into a tiny smile. "I'll try to remember that."

It feels weird but nice to have an older woman, the same age my mom would be, comforting and encouraging me.

HOURS LATER I'M STANDING IN THE SAME SPOT. THIS time, I'm wearing a floaty green dress, almost the color of the sea we swam in around Moni Island. Strappy block-heeled sandals and dangly earrings complete the ensemble.

I hope I look like an engaged, professional woman and not a dress-up doll.

Ajax has been busy all day. We haven't had time to check in with each other and make sure our stories mesh perfectly. It helps that I've met most of his family already so there are no big introductions to get through.

I get the feeling he's avoiding me. It's all my fault. I can't blame him after my epic failure last night. With everything happening, the disconnect with Ajax is adding to the queasiness in my stomach.

This party must go perfectly. We must convince everyone we're really engaged . . . to prevent the arranged marriage. And I must succeed in the rebranding plan. These are the reasons I came to Greece in the first place.

When Ajax walks onto the patio a half hour later dressed in linen slacks, and an open-necked white linen shirt, my heart thumps loudly. A full-scale dialogue plays out in my head.

This is my man.

Your temporary man, you mean.

Shut up. He's mine today.

Don't get attached, Bridget. Remember your rule.

Ajax greets his family and friends as he makes his way towards me. I try to relax, but end up crossing one leg, then the other leg, then finally sitting at the edge of my seat like a bird on a wire.

The old Bridget would have had her phone out snapping photos of everyone and everything. Making a video of Ajax in his fine clothes and his fine dimpled smile shaking hands and hugging his guests.

But I don't have my phone. I was too ashamed to go find it this morning. Plus, I'm not ready to read all the messages I know will be there from my family.

"You look lovely," Ajax says politely. He reaches into one of his pockets. "Here's your phone."

"Thanks." I slip it into my purse without looking at it.

He bends his head toward mine. "You okay with everything here?" He indicates the screen and my laptop set up on the table.

I nod. "It's going to be a great party."

"Bridge?"

"Yes?" My heart leaps inside my chest.

"This isn't fake to me, you know."

I blink. "I know. Me either." It's the best I can do.

We stare at each other. He's waiting for me to say more.

Say something, I shout at myself. Tell this gorgeous, sweet, caring man that you love him.

Before I can speak, his father appears.

"There you two are. Come on and meet someone special to our family."

Ajax's brow is creased with his annoyance at his father's interruption. Or maybe at me for failing to speak up fast enough.

I cover my nerves with a big smile I learned in acting class. "Of course, Christos, I would love to meet anyone special to the family."

"Well then." Christos leads me and Ajax to a table. An older man and woman flank the most beautiful, breath-taking young woman. A woman I recognize, except I didn't know she could look like *this*! A true Greek goddess — Aphrodite, Artemis, and Athena wrapped in one.

"This is Mr. and Mrs. Galanis. And meet Iona Galanis."

Holy smokes!

I step backward. Straight into Ajax's broad chest. He catches me before I trip on his shoe.

I glance upwards to say thanks, but his gaze is focused entirely on the stunning beauty. The woman who was supposed to be his real fiancée today at this engagement party.

OMG, I am stealing her engagement party. I cover my face with my hands. None of my acting lessons can help me right now.

Iona's easy smile and sparkling green eyes greet Ajax like they've known each other forever. Which they kind of have.

Ajax reaches over to shake her parents' hands and then to give her a kiss on the cheek.

"I almost didn't recognize you," he says.

She nods, "I get that a lot."

"This is Bridget," he says bringing me forward.

I don't know what I expected, but Iona gives me a genuine smile. "Congratulations, to you both," she says.

"Thank you," Ajax says heartily.

"Yes, thank you," I try to say aloud, but nothing comes out of my mouth.

Iona gives me a quizzical look. "Bridget and I have met. Didn't she tell you?"

"Um . . . no, she didn't. Where did you guys meet?" Ajax's hand presses my lower back.

I take a deep breath. "In town. Hey, I'm sorry folks, I must go set up for the presentation."

"I'm very interested in your ideas for the olive oil, Bridget."

I want to dislike her . . . but there's nothing to dislike. She's perfect.

Iona's father beams at his daughter. "Tell Ajax about the farm you're looking at buying."

Ajax raises his eyebrows. "You're buying a farm?"

She nods like a queen. Regal and poised.

As I shuffle off to the table where my laptop sits, I leave Iona and Ajax discussing farming methods, their heads getting closer and closer together, their foreheads almost touching the way ours were a few minutes ago.

Side by side, they look perfect together. A matching pair.

It's amazing how much can change in five minutes.

Ajax has eyes for only one person right now. And it isn't me!

Chapter Thirty-Eight

AJAX

People say men lack emotions. Or men don't show emotions. Or men don't identify with their emotions.

I'm here to tell you that men feel as deep or deeper than women.

Bridget did not respond to my declarations of love, not once, or twice, but *three* times. My heart feels like she's holding it in her fist and squeezing it tightly.

Anything would have been better than her silence.

"Are you okay?" Iona appears next to me with two glasses of wine. She hands me one.

After discussing her purchase of a farm of her own, I'd walked off to process my thoughts about Bridget and what it meant that she didn't tell me she'd met Iona. Or that she's working at the theater with Iona. There seems to be a lot of stuff Bridget hasn't told me. Maybe I was wrong to think we were growing closer.

I cast away these hurtful thoughts and turn to the woman next to me.

"I'm fine. I think." No sense hiding the truth from someone whose family has known me since I was in diapers.

For the next half hour, Iona and I chat about everything from climate change issues to ways to diversify our olive farms by planting other kinds of fruit-bearing trees.

They're my favorite topics and soon we're sitting down drawing maps on a napkin using a pen that we retrieved from the Guest Book table.

Bridget is a couple of tables away. I can't get a good read on her as her back is turned.

Iona must see my gaze shifting over to Bridget often because she asks, "Is your fiancée okay with us talking like this?"

The way she says the word "fiancée" — as if she wants to put air quotes around the word — makes me ask impulsively, "Does it bother you that I'm with Bridget? I know our parents wanted something different for us."

She shakes her long, honey-colored hair back. It's the same long hair. The same smile. The same green eyes of the girl I knew in high school.

The only thing that's changed about Iona is her sense of confidence. She's got that through the roof now. But then, who has a lot of confidence in high school? I sure didn't.

She smiles the wide-open smile I remember. Sits back tall and looks me straight in the eye. "I always had a crush on you."

The pen falls out of my hand. "You did?" I scramble under the table to retrieve it. "You were always snarky towards me."

Her laugh is deep and friendly. "I was a fool. I figured if you wouldn't notice me as I was, I would play the mean girl, to get your attention. It was later that I realized you weren't like other guys. You didn't find the mean girl interesting."

I stare at her. "That would be an accurate statement."

"I owe you an apology then." She stretches out a hand and I shake it. "That's okay. But you didn't answer my question."

"I'm not upset. Our parents had a crazy idea, trying to plan an arranged marriage for us."

"Cool." I sigh with relief.

"But I was disappointed to hear you're engaged to someone else."

My head snaps up and I lock eyes with her.

She shrugs. "My father and your father made it all about the farm and the olive oil."

"Yeah," I say nodding my head. "An arranged marriage of convenience."

"But for me, it was more than that. If we're being straightforward, I see you as the kind of man I want to create a life with. Farming aside. We have basically everything in common. And I respect you."

I rub one of my eyebrows. "Huh." This is awkward. I never gave Iona a second thought. But seeing her in front of me now, hearing what she's saying, I'm more aware of Bridget's rejections of me and my love.

"They say, *love those who love you back*.'" Iona says a bit forlorn. "I guess I have to find someone who loves me back."

I stand up to leave before my thoughts go trekking down that horrible rabbit hole. Not that loving Iona is horrible. But loving anyone but Bridget feels wrong.

"I'm sorry. I've got to go help my fiancée. We can chat later." I push back my chair and hurry away.

The thought of not being with Bridget is agonizing. But how can I make her see that we belong together? I know she loves me even if she won't say it. Or admit it.

Chapter Thirty-Nine

BRIDGET

The Greeks know a thing or two about throwing a party. I'm too nervous to eat much but my stomach rumbles at the delicious scents coming from the earthenware bowls of moussaka, the baked eggplant and lamb meal that looks like shepherd's pie and tastes even better, as it's loaded with spices I can't name.

While everyone digs in, I'm frozen in my seat. I can see Ajax and Iona, heads bent together, talking nonstop, smiling, laughing, and looking perfect together. They are the real couple. They are the ones we should be celebrating.

What was I thinking of infiltrating this Greek family? With my whole fake fiancé idea just so my best friend wouldn't marry someone else, and I'd lose him forever. This scheme sure has back-fired on me.

Iona is perfect for Ajax. Anyone can see that.

I bend my head and fiddle with the settings on my laptop, making sure the presentation is good to go. Blood pounds in my temples.

A deep fear stirs like a storm cloud inside my chest. This ache is like nothing I've ever felt before. I feel afraid. But I don't know exactly what I am afraid of.

I open and close my documents. The graphs, the images for their rebranded products, and the TikTok screens I've downloaded. Everything to show a new way to increase their revenue base. Nothing needs fixing or rearranging. I'm wasting time.

I tell myself when I look up, Ajax and Iona will have gone their separate ways. And I'd be able to breathe easier. It's not as if my entire life revolves around this man.

It does not, I tell myself forcefully.

I am strong. I am independent. I am . . . a sob sticks in my throat.

I look up, and they're still close together. Talking in a heart-to-heart manner.

Iona's eyes are wide and beautiful, even from this far away.

Now he's leaning closer, gazing into her eyes. Oh God, I can't take this.

A stake is driving itself into my heart.

Is this what jealousy feels like? How do people deal with this emotion? It's dark and sad and scary all at once. Like a goddess gone berserk ready to release hail and lightning bolts.

If I didn't have to do this presentation, I'd go pack my bags right now.

"Bridget, you're the guest of honor. Do you want to walk around a bit before the presentation?"

Ajax slides into a seat next to me and leans forward. When he sees the tears hovering in my eyes, he pulls me close. "What's wrong?"

I shake my head. I can't be *that* woman who breaks down crying over a conversation she's totally imagined in her head. Not when I must get up in front of everyone and discuss their future.

"Everything's okay," I tell my fake fiancé. My lips set themselves into a tight smile. If he can read between the lines, he'd understand.

"When should we start the presentation?" I ask, wiping a sheen of moisture off my forehead, dabbing so as not to mess up my makeup.

He glances at his ancient watch. "Right now, okay? So you can relax and enjoy the party."

I nod. "Yes, it's fine." The sun has started setting behind the trees so there's no glare on the laptop screen.

Ajax stands up and bangs his water glass with a fork.

When the lawn has quieted down, Ajax bends over and whispers in my ear, asking if I want to join him. I stand up, flitting out the skirt of my emerald dress.

"Friends and family, my fiancée, Bridget Walker, has reconfigured the Christos Farm brand story and we are going to share it with you now. I think you all will agree we need a new image. And thank goodness my future bride has developed the best."

Loud clapping and cheers ensue. Ajax slides into the seat next to mine and throws his hands up in the air in my direction, "Ladies and gentlemen, please meet marketing genius, Bridget Walker."

I smile at the gathering, praying no one notices my distress.

My eyes travel the width of the tent. Papa and Mama Christos are center stage. She has a kind look on her face. He is all curiosity and expectation, leaning forward on his elbows waiting for me to speak. Elena is seated at their table. She waves at me. I smile back at her.

I exhale loudly, too loudly, and the sound catches on the small mic clipped to my collar. It echoes around the space.

People chuckle. Some call out encouragement, maybe recognizing I'm nervous.

I don't get nervous on the stage when it's time to perform. So why is this different? Maybe because so much is at stake.

I feel a strong hand slipping into my hand that is resting on the table.

I look down into the handsome features of the man I have fallen in love with.

I clear my throat and begin.

The presentation opens with my favorite slide. The drawing I had an artist create for the new image of Christos Oil. A simple olive branch centered below an image of Aegina's port lit up in the background. It is distinctively Aegina's port where bottles are shipped out, but also where the oil is produced.

Next is a picture of the entire clan I took today when they all arrived for the party. A lot of "ohhs" and "ahhs" greet that slide as they look around and point at each other.

"The Christos family origin story. It starts with your great-great-grandparents who cleared the land, planted the olive trees, and pressed the olives into the oil we call Christos Oil today. But there's more to this delicious olive oil than meets the eye. Consumers don't know and can't see all the efforts made to create a product that not only adds to their health, but helps to save the planet, too. We're going to change that. We want to show them that Christos Oil has enormous *arete*!"

A loud cheer goes up and I smile. So far so good.

With each slide showing an aspect of the business from the planting, to the pruning and harvesting, pressing and the final product, the air grows charged with feelings. I'm taking everyone down memory lane. They're remembering how they got here. Why the olive oil is memorable not only to them, but why others would think so, too.

At least I'm hoping these are the feelings I'm evoking. I can't be sure. Not one person has said a word or asked a question as I continue through the slides.

There are a few laughs when I show one of Ajax driving the tractor with Christos pointing out something to him. Ajax is about ten and he's smiling, looking as cocky as only a ten-year-old driving a tractor can look.

"The most important thing about Christos Olive Oil," I

conclude, "is that it represents a family's efforts. And it's made right here in Aegina. That's why it'll be up to you all to get the message out about this great product. And your island. I've drawn up a plan for how you will do so."

Everyone is staring. Some with frowns, some quizzically.

"We will bombard social media with content showing you all at work creating the oil. We will show your faces, your hands, your hard work. And your connections to the land and to each other."

A low murmur hums across the lawn.

"Let me give you some examples of content I've created so you can see what I have in mind."

I quickly go to the sites and open drafts of saved content.

A drone video of Ajax and his father in the fields that I shot. With upbeat music. A reel of photos from around the island with trending sounds. A video of the irrigation system with squiggly arrows explaining how it works. A photo montage of the farm.

I display the olives up close in a series of photos taken over the past six weeks. The content took a long time to put together, but I'm proud of it. It's some of my best work. Maybe because they mean more to me than just a product promotion.

"I've set up social media accounts for Christos Olive Oil on all the main sites," I explain to the gathering. "You can start adding photos and videos right away. I urge you to snap or record anything you think is critical to the growth and development of the products, but also the fun and beauty of the island." I glance around the faces, looking for a reaction.

"Um . . . thank you for listening! I'm happy to answer any questions." I finish and sit down. Why aren't they clapping or smiling or . . . something!

Ajax's warm hand is on my lower back protectively. "Any questions?" I ask hesitantly. No one is saying a word. I feel bee stings of nerves dancing on my spine.

"Um . . . yes, Bridget, thank you." Ajax's father stands up. "That was very interesting."

Iona claps her hands. "I thought it was excellent," she smiles at me.

I swallow hard. "Thank you."

Ajax looks around the room with confusion on his face. "What's wrong?"

A hundred voices shatter the silence.

"I can't do TikkyTok," says one aunt.

"I don't want pictures of my hands on the social media," says an uncle holding up his hands and waving them around. "They've got scars all over them."

His wife flaps his hands down onto her lap. "I love your hands."

"Who's going to do all that social media posting?" asks a younger cousin of Ajax's. "Is it going to be where my friends can see it? I don't want them seeing my grandfather online."

Papa Christos shakes his head. "Bridget, the labels for our new bottles are a nice addition to Christos Olive Oil. But I'm afraid we don't want to be exploited on the internet. Not like this. It's not who we are."

Exploited? What is he talking about?

Mama Christos nods. "Yes, dear. I thought you'd see we love our peace and tranquility. We don't want to dance on TikTok."

I shake my head. "You don't have to dance," I whisper. "You don't have to post your hands if you don't like that," I say to the uncle who is hiding his hands under the table. Just like I wish I could hide under this table.

My legs are shaking hard. Ajax rests a hand on one thigh. It helps me to calm down, but only a little.

Iona stands up and looks at me. "If I may speak?"

I nod at her to go ahead.

"Bridget has some fine ideas. Like the rebranding of the bottles. I love the image of the olive branch and Aegina's port. Don't you all?"

Low murmurs of agreement pick up volume around the room.

"I understand you don't want to use the Internet to connect with your audience. Your consumers, I mean. There are other ways to connect with them."

"Like how?" asks Mr. Christos.

Iona glances at me again. I stare at her wide-eyed. What can I do? I have to nod and smile. "Sure, please share." Inside, my nerves are wrecked.

"I've been looking into ways the people of Aegina can develop deeper connections with our visitors," Ionia says. "And one way I think will work for us is agritourism."

"What's that?" someone shouts. "Speak up louder."

I look on in horror as Iona Galanis hijacks my plans for the company that I've worked so long and hard on.

Iona moves closer to the table.

"Agritourism is where we create ways for tourists to interact with the growth and production of our farm products. So for olive oil on Christos Farm, we can offer tours of the farm. Visitors can help with the harvests and with the pressing of the oil.

"Tourists want to be educated and involved. And they can purchase their bottles of oil afterward. Most of them will take their own photos and videos and post them to their own social media accounts anyway. You'll still get exposure online; you just don't have to do it yourself."

She glances at me. "Right?"

I nod helplessly. "Yes."

"Baby steps, people," Iona grins at the crowd, most of whom have known her all her life. They smile and seem to relax.

"Social media postings help tremendously to get the word out about a product," Iona continues, speaking like she's had this idea in her head for a long time. "Bridget's content is amazing. Trust me, I spend way too much time on social media."

The older folks laugh. The younger ones nod their heads. Iona has connected with everyone.

She has them hanging on her every word. "Christos Farm

should use Bridget's posts to get its marketing started. It'll get lots of attention with the great oil you produce combined with the agritours."

Everyone claps. Glasses are raised as they toast Iona and me. But mostly Iona.

But I shouldn't be surprised. These are her people. This is her culture. She knows it better than me. She knows they wouldn't want to broadcast their lives on the internet. She knows they're self-sufficient islanders who love their privacy but are proud of their farms and its products. How could I imagine I'd understand a different culture and know what its citizens want in such a short time?

I should have asked Iona for her input instead of focusing on keeping her and Ajax apart. I had plenty of time while we worked at the Municipal Theater. But I was too busy hiding behind my insecurities.

Iona winds down her spiel with a wink at the crowd. "This is a family affair so we should all be involved. Even you Tio Sebastian with your naughty hands."

Laughter ripples through the crowd.

It's the way she said, "we," that makes my breath catch in my throat.

People clap loudly for Iona. They call out her name. She smiles and waves her hands at them to stop. "This is not about me today. I just wanted to add my ideas to Bridget's."

"Thanks, Bridget," the family members call out one by one.

I nod and mumble, "You're welcome."

I glance over at Ajax to see what he's thinking. But he's staring at Iona Galanis, who is flitting from one family member to the next as they ask questions about agritourism and how it can benefit the company.

"I'll be right back," I murmur and slip away to the side doors. I race down the hall, grab the door handle with shaking hands, and seek refuge in my cool dark bedroom. I kick off my shoes and throw myself onto the bed, covering my mouth so no one can hear me crying.

It's like déjà vu from last night.

I failed. The presentation failed. The fake fiancé relationship failed. And Iona's idea to introduce agritourism to the olive farm is brilliant. It just never occurred to me.

With the way Ajax was staring at Iona, he feels the same way.

I close my eyes, feeling tears dripping down my eyelashes.

The only thing standing in the way of Ajax and Iona's future is me.

I have my rules for a reason. Don't get attached. Because look what happens when you do. You end up crying after watching the man you love fall in love with someone else.

Life does that to you. Yanks out the happiness right from under your feet.

Chapter Forty

AJAX

I don't know where Bridget has disappeared. I check the garden and the other tents where the food and drinks are set up. I ask Elena and Mama, but no one's seen her.

Meanwhile, Iona is leading me to talk to her parents to explain that the piece of land she wants to buy is a good idea. But I can't focus on her or her family right now. I need to find Bridget. I need to get away from them.

"Ajax, isn't our daughter a genius?" Mr. Galanis asks as if I haven't known Iona all my life.

I smile politely and shake his hand. "She is sir. She has great ideas. I'm sure you're happy to have Iona home." I'm talking, but my eyes are diving over their shoulders in search of Bridget.

Iona laughs. "They'll get tired of me soon. I'm constantly talking about business ideas with them. They want to keep the taverna the exact same way it's been for twenty years since I was a little girl."

"What's wrong with that?" Mr. Galinas asks. "It's tradition."

I nod. "Tradition is important, true."

Mr. Galanis looks at me strangely. "I thought you believed in breaking traditions."

I mumble something about seeing it from all angles and make my escape.

I head inside the house. She's not in the kitchen or family room or anywhere else. I see a light coming from under her bedroom door. I knock. She may have just left the light on. Who knows?

I'm surprised to hear noises inside. "Bridget, can I come in? Are you okay?"

No answer. I shake the doorknob. It's locked.

I hear her talking on the phone. It sounds like she's crying.

"Bridget!" I call out sharply.

I rattle the doorknob. "Can I talk to you please?"

A few long minutes pass by as I wait for her to let me in.

I cross my arms on my chest. An ominous dread fills me.

Finally, she slides the door open and steps backward.

She's still wearing her beautiful silk dress, but it's wrinkled and creased.

"What's wrong?" I ask.

She closes the door behind me and gestures for me to follow her outside to her balcony where her phone sits on the table.

Before I can say a word, she starts off. "I want you to know how grateful I am that I came here. I did my best to come up with a marketing plan for the family, but I messed up. I didn't consider the things they value the most. What you value the most."

"What . . . ?" She raises a hand.

"Please let me finish."

"I misjudged everything. My focus was on digital social branding, but you guys want a more interactive experience and that's great. I'm just not the person for that job. I failed you. I failed your family. But you do have Iona. She is the one you want and need."

"No, Bridget . . . can I speak now?"

She shakes her head. "There's more."

I reach out a hand to touch her and she steps backward again.

"I think I should leave. I've finished my presentation. It wasn't what they wanted, and well . . . "

Now, I interrupt. "So, your plan didn't fit the family. No big deal. It's not a surprise that Iona came up with the perfect idea for them. She's known them all her life. She knows Aegina and its people. You've been here only six weeks, Bridget. Long enough for a peek into our lives. Not long enough to know what Iona knows because she's part of the culture."

"That's just it. She belongs here. I don't. You looked like you were having so much fun with her today."

"I have fun with you, Bridget. More fun than I've ever had with anyone. Please don't compare."

"You're not having fun now. Look at us. We're fighting."

I take her shoulders, and bend down to look into her sad eyes. "We're going to have fights. I promise you that. But we're also going to work through them. Because we love each other."

She shakes her head from side to side. "I should be leaving soon."

My voice explodes. "Why? We still have two more months of your trip."

She literally jumps backward.

"Sorry, I don't mean to shout."

"No, it's okay. You're mad, I understand. I would be mad, too."

"What are you talking about?"

"I'm talking about us. We should never have come up with this crazy plan to fool everyone that we're engaged. The only people we really fool are ourselves."

"Wait, what? I thought we were talking about marketing plans." Fear, cold and heavy grips my heart. "For the record, it was real to me. I don't feel fooled."

"Well, you should," she says defiantly, looking at me with tear drops hanging on her eyelashes.

"If it's all so wrong, why are you crying?" I challenge her.

"That's the point. I don't want to cry over you."

I inhale sharply.

"I've cried enough in my life. Enough! Do you hear me?" This time it's her voice that's rising in volume. "I'm not going to cry over you or anyone else!"

She's pacing and turns to glare at me.

"I'm sorry, Bridget. I don't know why you're so angry at me. What did I do? Why has everything suddenly changed?"

She stops pacing. "It's always been like this. I cannot do relationships. Especially when I can see so clearly that you and Iona would be perfect together. I cannot get in the way of that future."

"What the . . . me and Iona? There is no *me and Iona*."

"But there can be. She is everything you want and need. Not to mention she's gorgeous. And your families already approve."

"I don't care about any of that." I reach out for her hand. "Bridget, I love you. That's what's most important."

"Oh, I forgot to add," Bridget says drily. "Iona *lives* here. I don't."

I balk. Drop my hand.

She glares at me, her eyes like knives sticking her last sentence into me for good measure. "Did you actually think I would move to this island, Ajax?"

I take two steps toward her. Her hand pushes me back.

"I hoped," I say. "I prayed."

"That was never part of our plan. The plan was for me to come here, be your fake fiancé so you wouldn't have to marry a stranger, and try to help your family with a rebranding of the olive oil. Our plan was never for me to stay."

A noise draws our attention away.

I look up to find my father, mother, Elena, and Iona standing by the olive trees closest to the balcony.

Mama has a hand over her mouth. Elena's eyes are wide open, darting between me and Bridget.

And Papa. His face is the worst. Disappointment clouds his eyes. He's shaking his head, his chin drooping onto his chest like he can't look at me.

"Papa," I call out.

He takes Mama's hand and tucks it under his, giving me and Bridget the saddest shake of his head I've ever seen. Papa never does sad. He's angry, stubborn, or fiery. Never sad. They all turn and walk away while I watch with my hand over my heart.

"I've ruined everything," Bridget cries. "Now you see why I have to leave."

For the first time since I've known her, I feel anger toward her. Or maybe it's anger toward myself.

I've hurt my family. Lost Papa and Mama's trust for sure. Maybe even Elena's too. Iona Galanis will tell everyone what a jerk I am.

And I wagered everything on Bridget falling in love with Aegina and me.

That's never going to happen. I see that now.

"You're going to be okay, Ajax," Bridget says softly. "You can start over with Iona. You'll have an investor to inject capital into the farm and save all your trees. And you guys can take your time and fall in love right here."

"Thank you for planning my entire life for me." My words are bitter, but I can't help it. "You're only leaving because you're afraid to commit. Why won't you admit that? You're using Iona Galanis to hide your true feelings."

Daggers shoot at me from her dark glare.

I sigh as the anger seeps out of me. How can I stay angry at her? "Look, I know I can't force you to love me or to stay here with me. It's like trying to force an olive tree to bear more fruit when it's giving you its best. But I'm willing to try. I want to give us my best try."

"Leaving you *is* my best try," she says.

My heart races to my throat. I want to shout, "Please don't

leave me. Please don't run away. I love you so much. Stay with me." But then I'd never be sure if she stayed because she loved me or if she stayed because I begged her to. In that case, she'd just leave later. It's better to know now.

"I think we both know what I'm saying, Ajax."

"Please Bridget, I know you love me."

She shakes her head. "Not enough."

"That's not true." I grab her hands. Tears are falling fast. Sobs wrack my body. I'm gripping her hand so tightly she can't peel away.

"I'm sorry Ajax. I'm so sorry. I should never have come."

I don't know if you can hear a heart breaking in two. But at this moment, I hear mine. It shatters into a hundred pieces like Humpty Dumpty falling off the wall.

I let go of her hands and stagger backward.

How could I have been so wrong?

Chapter Forty-One

BRIDGET

Do you ever feel in the moment of doing something that you're making a huge mistake, but you can't stop yourself from making it? As if you're on this path of self-destruction and you can't get off?

Well, that's how I feel watching the shock on Ajax's face as I obliterate our relationship — or whatever the hell it was. By the time I'm done telling him that I wish I'd never come, or something like that, I know I've lost him for good.

A part of me feels that I had to hammer that last nail in the coffin of our friendship like I dare not leave any openings for fear I'd struggle with closure.

The thing is that after all that sound and fury is released, I'm left feeling absolutely nothing but emptiness.

It's close to the feeling of loss I thought I'd never have to feel again. That aching, empty, hollow hole in my heart where ice poured in so I could fill it with something.

Ajax stares at me, his face drained of color. His eyes bleak and sad and the embers of light dying out right before my eyes.

He walks through my room and out the door. He doesn't say goodbye. I hope he goes to Iona now. Or later. Whenever, as long as he does. She can help them save the farm and be the wife he wants. That's what I'm thinking. But do I really mean it?

Yes. Ajax will live happily ever after with a girl from his island and I will return to Portland and . . . help Ava with her gelateria. Be there for Daisy when she comes home from college. Supervise and chaperone Emerald's senior dances and prom. Keep Emmie from making mistakes with Jackson, or another boy who might want to break her heart.

I will let Corrine know she can skip Greece and maybe I'll meet her in Portugal. Yeah, that's what I'll do. I'll leave Aegina, go to Portugal, spend time with my sister, and recover the real Bridget Walker.

Leave this fake girl behind. The one who believed she was falling in love with her best friend but who could never really be in love with anyone. Because as everyone knows, especially *me*, I don't do relationships.

And now, for sure I never will.

Chapter Forty-Two

BRIDGET

I spend the rest of the evening in my room. Binge watching *Vampire Diaries* on my iPad. Watching Damon Salvatore demolish a few necks and hearts works fine for easing the pain throbbing all over my body.

A tiny part of me — the budding flower in a sea of toxicity — hoped Ajax would return.

But no, I shut that door good and solid. Hope does not bloom when I've thrown acid on it. Not to mention I'm too ashamed to face his mother, father, and sister.

How can I explain that I didn't mean to hurt them?

Especially little Elena who was so happy to have me here. In our weeks together, I learned about her dyslexia and helped her every day with reading the printouts for the trees. She'd make an excellent farmer one day.

I fall asleep hungry and sad and locked in a death grip of emotions I don't want to feel.

The next morning, I wake up sweaty and sticky because I forgot to turn on the a/c and had somehow managed to wrap my body like a mummy in the blankets.

As I struggle to disentangle my legs and arms, everything I said to Ajax comes flooding back into my mind. I shiver with the shame of it all. I was mean.

Since when am I mean? And to him?

THE WAY I TOLD AJAX WE'RE OVER. THE WAY HE looked. The way I said I wish I'd never come. Mostly I told him he should go to Iona because she's the right girl for him.

They say, "Be careful what you think because thoughts become reality."

Well, in my case, it was more than thoughts. I willed him to go find Iona and make her his very own.

I rub my eyes to wake up. Getting showered and dressed is easy as it's late and everyone's gone down to either clean up from yesterday or start the typical farm day.

Once I'm dressed, I flip open my phone and check the time difference. It's still too early to call anyone in Maine. Corrine is not due to fly to Portugal until later this week.

I shut my phone off and head downstairs to find a cup of coffee. I need to apologize to Ajax's entire family for coming here under false pretenses.

Just as I'm sitting down at the table in the family room — because I'm too nervous or too cowardly to go outside and run into Ajax or his mother and father — the man himself strides into the room, pushing his grey bandana off his forehead until it hangs around his neck like a flag.

He stops mid-walk. His dark eyes flit over me, then stop when they reach the floor. "Hi, Bridget."

"Hi." My voice is a croaky frog. I sip the coffee, holding the mug in front of me protectively.

Silence overwhelms us. I jump for the easiest thing to say. "Don't worry. I'll be leaving as soon as I can. Will you please tell your parents and Elena I said, I'm sorry."

He nods. "They're not here right now. They took Elena to the beach."

"She deserves it. She works hard around here."

"We all do. They needed a break today."

"I'm sorry," I mumble, tears hitting the backs of my eyelids like hail on a windshield.

I blink hard. Don't cry in front of him. Don't break down.

His eyes shoot up to my face. "You don't have to leave. I get it, we broke up, if we were even together, but you don't have to leave." His tone is cold. A side of him I've never seen before.

"Thanks," I say as graciously as I can. "I appreciate it."

I surprise myself with my next words. "I'm going to catch the ferry and head over to Athens for a few days like we talked about doing after the presentation."

He's staring. Not speaking.

"If that's okay with you."

He nods his head. "You don't need my permission."

"Right. Okay, then. Can I get a ride to the port?"

He drops his hands. "Whatever you want."

"Fine."

"Fine, which ferry are you catching?"

I stand up leaving my full mug of coffee on the table. "The next one."

I hurry from the room before I break down. I know I caused this, but I can't handle feeling unloved by the person who declared his love for me yesterday.

Two hours later, I'm standing on the top level of the large car ferry watching the beautiful fishing port of Aegina town grow smaller and smaller until we turn the corner of the island and I can't see the fishing boats or Ajax's truck parked next to his Uncle Theo's shop.

I've got a backpack of clothing, toiletries, and a laptop. I've got an Airbnb reservation in the middle of Athens near the Acropolis.

I'm determined to keep busy. To see Athens and its temples and statues.

A cool sea breeze whips the ends of my hair off my shoulder. I hug my arms around my body feeling bereft and alone.

By the time I get Corrine on the phone, I'm crying. The salty breeze does not help to dry the unstoppable tears.

"I broke up with him," I sob.

"You did what?" Corrine shouts in my ear. I don't turn on my camera because I don't want her to see how horrible I look. Tears, runny nose, and reddening eyes. A hot mess.

I hear Ava's voice in the background. "Is she okay?"

Corrine asks, "Ava wants to know if you're okay."

"No. Not at all. I feel like I lost my best friend."

"You did lose your best friend." It's Daisy's voice, loud and clear. "How could you break up with that awesome man?"

I gulp. "I don't know. I really don't know what happened."

Ava's voice now. "Break ups don't just happen, Bridge. You make them happen. So, what was it this time?"

"Please don't go there."

Ava's tone softens. "Okay, but why?"

She puts me on speaker, and I relay the whole sordid story — about Iona showing up looking like a Greek princess. How she and

Ajax would make a much better couple and how I felt like I was stealing away their chance of a real life romance.

"What did he do exactly? For you to end the relationship?" Emerald pipes up. "Did he cheat with Iona? Was he disrespectful to you? What?"

"He didn't do anything," I confess.

Daisy does her *tssk tssk* sound. "So you broke up with him over . . . what exactly?"

"Yeah, what?" three other voices ask.

I press the phone to my heart and stare at the sprawling city. Athens is only a forty-five-minute ferry ride from Aegina. But it's a whole world away. An entirely different country with its mega cruise ships docked in the port, the cargo ships unloading goods, and thousands of people scurrying along the docks.

"Whoa!"

"What is happening?" My sisters are yelling. "What's going on?"

I press the video icon and turn the phone around.

"You're not in Kansas anymore little sis," Ava says.

"Tell me about it."

"What's your plan now that you figged up a perfectly good relationship?" Daisy demands to know.

I look at my sisters. It's only a little after 7 a.m. their time. Yet, they're all dressed and getting ready to head out to summer jobs or to Ava's gelateria to continue fixing up the new venture.

"I'm sorry to hold you all up," I tell them. "I'm feeling so . . ."

"Dumb?" Emerald says without missing a beat.

"Emmie," Ava warns. "Don't speak to Bridget like that especially when she's in pain."

"Well, she caused her own pain."

Corrine sighs. "That's usually what people do, Em, they hurt themselves. It seems like our invincible warrior, Bridget, has taken a serious self-inflicted battle wound."

"Geez, I'm still here," I mutter.

"What is your plan, Bridget?" Ava asks.

"I don't really know," I cry.

Corrine grabs the phone on their end.

"I'm coming, Bridge. Just hold on."

I let out a huge sigh. "Really? When?"

Corrine checks her calendar. "I leave here on Thursday. I'll drop off my stuff in my apartment in Portugal, then head straight for Athens. I'll be by your side by Saturday at the latest."

That's five days. I can wander around Athens for five days without expiring in a heap of tears. I think.

"Okay, hurry. I need you."

"But wait, Bridge, why don't you just come home? We can change your ticket to return sooner than the end of summer."

I shake my head. "No, I came all the way out here. I want to see Athens and other parts of Greece."

"But what about Aegina and Ajax and his family? You can't run out on them."

"I already did," I sigh.

Ava's shaking her head. "I was afraid this would happen." She looks at the others. "We hoped a trip abroad and a chance to know Ajax would make a difference."

"If you mean I'm still the one least likely to settle down, then yeah, I haven't changed much."

After we hang up, I gather my backpack and follow the other travelers off the ferry, across the wide dock and out into the steaming streets of Athens, Greece.

Hawkers selling sunglasses and wallets greet me outside the ferry gates. I'm surrounded by juice vendors, food trucks, and a line of taxis waiting to take cruise ship passengers on city tours.

I hand a driver my phone to show him the Airbnb I booked, and he waves me into the taxi.

The deeper into the city we drive, the more we're surrounded by tall buildings but also green parks. And ancient ruins!

They're everywhere! Towers, gates, walls, and columns.

They've sat here and watched the modern city develop around them for hundreds and hundreds of years. Like Ajax's favorite olive trees. Nature created them. Architects and builders created these monuments.

Athens is helping me feel like my problems and struggles are not as significant as I believed.

I wish Ajax was here so I could squeal with excitement and make him pose like a Greek god next to the ancient buildings.

A dark cloak of despair tightens around me.

What the hell did I do?

Why don't I feel better? I'm supposed to feel better now that we broke up and the lies are over. I should be feeling ecstatic. Carefree and single and happy.

None of those feelings are on my radar.

Instead, I feel sick. Physically sick. With an overpowering urge to call Ajax and say it was a mistake. I wasn't serious. I love him. Don't go to Iona. I'm willing to beg even.

Oh God, I press my eyelids down tightly to block out the image of Ajax kissing Iona. Hugging her close, his strong arms wrapped tightly around her so she can't get away the way I did.

But I can't do any of those things.

He'd think I was a whack job. The kind of person who cares so little for his feelings that I'm willing to destroy everything, then apologize.

And even if he forgives me and takes me back, I can't make any promises about a future together.

Chapter Forty-Three

AJAX

I didn't see this coming.

How could I not see this breakup coming? I know Bridget's personality. She's told me herself she can't commit to anyone.

Who am I to think I could make her change her personality? How could I be so arrogant and clueless as to what she was thinking and feeling?

I was so wrapped up in my own happiness, I thought I could carry her along; and convince her she was as happy as I was.

I was a fool. I'm still a fool. I just dropped her off at the ferry and didn't say a word as she got out and walked away.

Yeah, I stayed at the dock until I saw her board the ferry with my own eyes.

I thought she'd change her mind. I thought she'd turn around and come running back to me. Tell me she's wrong, tell me she loves me, and we will work through this mess.

But she didn't even glance over her shoulder. I'm sure she had no idea I sat in my truck waiting for her to come back.

When the ferry blew its horn a few times, raised its doors, and shut them tight, that was when I banged my fist on the steering wheel.

You idiot. How could you let her leave? You should have gone with her. As a friend. To be by her side in the big city. Instead, you let her go off alone because your pride hurts.

It's my heart that's aching, I argue with myself.

A loud rapping on my window yanks me out of my internal fight. "You gotta leave this spot. You can't park here."

It's the port security. "Yeah, yeah, I'm leaving," I say, knowing he's just doing his job.

The drive home is the worst drive I've ever taken. Memories of Bridget sitting by my side flit through my head. A nonstop montage of our day-to-day life.

In every memory, a love, deep and strong and real, invades my senses. Not just my mind. I can smell her jasmine scent in the jeep. I can see her brown eyes laughing at me. I can even feel how her hands felt when she slipped hers into mine and we cuddled on my sofa.

No one can replace Bridget. I wonder why she thinks anyone can.

Chapter Forty-Four

BRIDGET

For two days I wandered around Athens. I climbed the hill to the Acropolis. I admired the imposing Parthenon and the stunning Temple of Athena Nike. All this beauty and history and still I can't shake off my gloom.

Everywhere I look, everywhere I walk, memories of Ajax and his family flood my brain.

When a waiter offers me a glass of ouzo at the end of a meal, I see Mr. and Mrs. Christos pouring glasses of ouzo on my first day.

When I wander around the Archaeological Museum, I recall my and Ajax's visit to the tiny museum next to the Temple of Aphaia.

When I read about how the goddess Athena brought peace and prosperity to this magnificent city with her olive tree, I cry inside.

Still, I walk endlessly through the different boroughs of Athens. Sometimes I end up at a busy restaurant or a quiet taverna. But never do I run into the one person who could make this heartache go away.

He's so close. Just a short ferry ride away.

I ache to jump on the next boat and head back to Aegina. But what would it solve?

I'm alone with my thoughts. Not even one of Athens' stray kitty cats wants to be around a sad person.

"What's wrong with me?" I ask Ava on the phone one evening.

"Nothing is wrong with you. It takes a lot of courage to love someone."

"I used to be fearless," I say.

"There's a difference between being fearless and having courage."

"Hmmm," I ponder my older sister's words.

"It's easy to be fearless when you have nothing to lose. It takes courage to put your heart and soul into another's hands," Ava says gently.

"How do you do it? With Tyler?

She grins at me through the phone. "I have faith in myself."

"I thought you were going to say you have faith in him."

"I do. But first, I had to believe in myself. Who I am. What I stand for."

"Oh," I groan. "You have to *know* yourself."

Ava chuckles. "It's a cliché. But it's a cliché because it's true."

"How do you do it? This whole knowing yourself thing?"

She pauses. "You pay attention."

"To what?" I screech.

"To everything. Focus on what your heart connects with and go from there."

ON MY THIRD DAY IN ATHENS, I WAKE UP AND THINK, "Okay, today I will feel better. Today I will stop crying every five minutes and enjoy the beauty of Athens and maybe learn a few lessons in history along the way."

The empty hole widens inside me instead. I walk around like a zombie on cruise control. I snap photos of what I believe are the sights without really seeing them.

What I see is me and Ajax floating on the blue-green sea, our fingers touching, thinking we had all the time in the world.

I see him washing my feet and wrapping bandages around my insteps. Then piggybacking me so I wouldn't have to walk.

My mind is so far away, I stumble on the edge of an ancient boulder before I realize what I'm standing next to; a giant Roman amphitheater built into the side of the hill right below the Acropolis. How have I not seen this before?

I Google it immediately. The Odeon of Herodes Atticus. It's still being used for musical performances. Built in 161 A.D. by the philosopher Herodes Atticus for his wife after he lost her.

What an awesome tribute. This is what the books and movies call a grand gesture. Building a theater for your woman to show your love, is as grand as it gets.

I feel that strong urge for the hundredth time to call Ajax. To tell him about this amazing amphitheater.

I buy a ticket to enter the archaeological site. It's hundreds of years old but the Roman arches are still on display.

My heart skips a beat when I see the word *"Arete"* scrawled amongst other graffiti near the site.

I walk amongst the many steps that were the seats the ancient citizens of Athens sat on to watch plays and performances on the stage below.

I would love to see a performance here. To experience theater as it was invented. I make my way down the steps toward the large, round black circle that is the stage.

I climb up and gaze outward at the semi-circle of seats. People lounge on the steps eating lunch, or just hanging out, enjoying the blend of the past and the present.

I walk slowly around the perimeter of the black dais of one of the oldest theaters ever built. I'm stepping in the footsteps of actors from centuries ago. My heart beats faster.

I recite lines from one of my old plays. Acting is pretending. I pretend I am one of the ancient actors delivering lines before an audience of thousands of Greeks. My heartbeat accelerates.

Ava said I must focus on what my heart connects with and go from there.

My heart is leaping with excitement to be standing on this stage. The first smile of the past three days curves my lips.

I was happiest when I was on stage. Why did I stop acting? Why did I give up performing to take a seat in the audience?

I look at the sky. I don't expect to find any answers up there. What I see are birds spreading their wings wide as they sail on the air currents. Flying across the blue universe. They know where they're headed instinctively.

They trust in nature, the seasons, and their innate birdness to know what to do. And when to do it.

I need to do that. Trust in myself to know what I like and what I need.

Chapter Forty-Five

AJAX

I miss her so much I'm dying little deaths inside every day.

My family seems to understand what I'm going through. Over the past few days, they've rallied around me, trying to help me feel better. Except for Elena.

Papa had sighed and said he wished he'd never said she wouldn't last. Maybe he jinxed the whole thing.

Mama said Bridget needed her mother.

When I told her that Bridget's mother passed away when Bridget was thirteen, Mama said, that explained it. "Everyone needs their mother."

Elena blames me for Bridget leaving. "What did you do?" she cried when she found out Bridget left without saying goodbye.

"I don't know, sweetie."

Elena glared at me. "You know."

I shook my head. "I tried everything."

"You're not trying anything at all. You're giving up." She threw her dish towel at me and ran out of the room.

When I went to try and talk to her, Elena said bitterly, "Ajax was a hero. You're not. You're not doing anything to make her come back here. I love her."

"I love her too, squirt."

"Well then, go and get her."

"It's not that easy. She doesn't want to be with me."

Elena rolled her wet eyes. "You're being dumb. Of course, she wants to be with you. Anyone can see that."

Since I couldn't convince Elena of the reality of the adult world, I left her alone to brood and stay mad at me. Maybe I deserved it after all.

I check my phone constantly. For calls. Or texts.

The silence is a deep abyss. I'm holding on to the edge trying to not let myself fall over into it.

But what do you hold onto when there's nothing left?

Not a single flash of light from the farthest star can reach me. Everything is dark.

Until one day, I'm in the olive fields. There's been damage to a row of trees from a pest. Since we can't use pesticides, or since I refuse to, I'm trying other ways to rid the forest of this invasive species.

My phone rings and I grab it, hoping I'll see her name on the caller ID.

It's Tyler.

"Yo, dude, are you okay? Man, I heard the bad news. You guys broke up?"

I swear under my breath. "I guess it's official then if you heard it."

"So sorry, my man. I know you cared about her."

"What exactly have you heard? She won't call me, and I don't want to be the stalker friend."

"Well, Corrine, the middle sister, is heading to Athens today to meet up with Bridget."

I sigh with relief. I didn't realize how worried I'd been about Bridget being by herself in the city.

"I'm glad she'll have her sister for company. Although, I wish it was me going to her."

"Ajax."

"Yeah."

"Don't give up."

"What do you mean?"

"These sisters. The Walker women . . . they're awesome. All of them. They had a really messed up situation hit them at a young age. Ava says it affects all of them differently. She said Bridget is afraid to love and runs from it. It's her M.O."

I sigh. "Tell me something I don't know, dude."

"All I'm saying is don't give up on her. She needs you."

"I don't know about that."

"I heard you may be interested in another woman on Aegina."

I snort. "Fake news, dude. Bridget was jumping to conclusions. She's convinced Iona Galanis and I would be the perfect couple."

"Is she partly right?"

"No way. My heart belongs to Bridget."

Tyler is silent.

"What do you think I should do?"

Tyler doesn't respond again. He sounds like he's talking to someone in the background.

"Tyler?" I call out.

He returns to the phone. "If you love Bridget, you have to show her."

"What do you mean?"

"That's what Ava says. You must demonstrate it so loudly and so clearly that she can't miss the signs."

"I bought her an engagement ring, dude. I was going to ask her to be my real fiancée. After the party. But she left."

Tyler whispers in the background. I hear female voices squealing.

The next thing I know, Ava's shouting at me. "If you love

Bridget you have to go get her. She's in pain. She loves you. You're both being so . . . ."

"Stupid!" I hear a voice yelling in the background.

"It's not nice to call him names," Ava reacts immediately.

"Sorry," says the background voice. "Not sorry, though."

"She's right. I've been an idiot. My sister Elena said the same thing. I should have gone after Bridget right away. I think my pride was so hurt; I wasn't thinking straight. Not to mention I have no idea where she went."

Ava sighs. "Love can be difficult. The easy thing to do is to break up. It's much harder to stay and fight for what can be. But that's what you do if it's real love. I should know."

I grip the phone hard. "Are you telling me that I would not be harassing her if I go to Athens and convince her to come back to me?"

"Well . . . it depends on how you do it. With Bridget, you gotta make a convincing show of it."

"How do you know that?"

"I don't. But you must find a way to get through to her. And she loves a good show."

"Ahhh! I got it. Thank you. Make a spectacle of myself."

Ava laughs. "Remember when I created a *te amo* Tyler gelato and announced in front of everyone how much I loved that man?"

"Yeah, I was right there. With Bridget."

"You need to take your own Superman leap."

"That's what my baby sister was trying to tell me," I admit.

"Elena knows what she's talking about," Ava says. "Good luck. Corrine will be there by tomorrow morning."

Before we hang up, Ava gives me the address of their rental apartment.

"Thank you, Ava, and whichever other sister is in the background."

"That would be Daisy."

"Thanks, Daisy!" I shout.

"You're welcome, Ajax!" the voice shouts back.

"But I have one last question. Why do you want us to make it work if she can't stay in Aegina with me?"

"One step at a time," Ava says calmly. "Love conquers a lot. Maybe it can conquer that obstacle too."

We hang up. I wish I felt as optimistic as Ava and her sisters, that I could change Bridget's mind.

At that moment I see a small movement and catch sight of the enemy beetle scampering across the dirt. I drop down on my knees to investigate the bug situation, determined to protect my olives from any enemies and overcome all obstacles to keep what I love safe.

Chapter Forty-Six

BRIDGET

Corrine has always been the smart sister. She masters languages quickly, has a photographic memory, and can code while knitting a fancy sweater.

Her talents are so numerous that she's never known what she wanted to do in life because she's talented at so many things.

The only thing she's terrible at is choosing a good guy.

As smart as she is, she misses every single red flag waved in her face and always ends up with the bad boy in the crowd.

Now, watching her long brown legs stride toward me in jean shorts and an off-the-shoulder top, I realize my little sister — well younger by two years — has found two of her favorite type of men on the plane — alpha males with attitude. The kind of men Ava and I would *not* be interested in.

Tall, athletic, designer sunglasses on top of their heads, one with colorful neck tattoos and the other with spiky hair, both carrying expensive leather bags and laughing with Corrine.

As the three of them get closer, I hang back, not sure what's going on because loud shrieks of "they're here!" come from all parts of the arrivals area.

Corrine ducks around the crowd and beelines towards me.

"What's going on?" I grab my sister in a hug so tight I hear a couple of her bones cracking.

"Ouch, woman," she grimaces. "I missed you too."

We hold each other at arm's length and laugh. Then hug again, the typical airport greeting that happens everywhere in the world.

"Who are those . . . scary looking men?" I ask.

Corrine grins like she's a cat and I've asked her who are those two yummy canaries.

"Footballers," she smirks. "A whole team was on my flight."

"And you ended up with two of them?"

She tick tocks her tongue on the roof of her mouth making her signature clicking sound. "No, Bridget Walker. One is for you."

My mouth drops open so fast, Corrine laughs. "Get a grip, I was kidding. I know you're having man troubles."

"I think they sent me the wrong sister."

She scoffs. "No, the right one. Ava would have been all touchy feely. Daisy would have cried or complained. And Emerald would have told you to think about the environment instead. At least with me, you can have some fun."

"I'm not up for fun," I grumble.

"We'll see. There they are," Corrine says as her two footballers stroll through the parted sea of autograph seekers and approach us.

"Danielo and Salvador. This is my sister, Bridget."

We shake hands and their grips tell me they're used to fighting, whether only on the field is yet to be seen. Total alpha males if I ever saw some.

More footballers exit the baggage area followed by even louder screams of excitement. "Wow! What team do you play for?"

"The best one," says the tattooed Danielo.

He puts a hand on my lower back and steers me outside the wide airport doors. I see Salvador has done the same thing with

Corrine. I try to walk fast so he's not touching me, but his hand is glued to my side. "It's okay, Bridget, I got you."

"Great," I murmur.

"We're catching a ride with them," Corrine says brightly, her guy Salvador walking like he's a bodyguard.

A large black limo appears out of nowhere and the next thing I know, we're being herded inside the cavernous vehicle.

"Corrine . . . um . . ."

"It's okay, Bridget. We'll take good care of you," Danielo says.

Someone pops a bottle of champagne and techno music blares from speakers. A glass of bubbly is thrust into my hand. I weakly say thanks.

I'm missing Ajax more than ever surrounded by these macho athletes. I want my sweet wonderful darling man, who is as rugged as these dudes, but nicer. I'd bet on it.

Corrine leans forward. "It's okay. I spoke to both their mothers by video call before we took off from Lisbon. They told their sons to be nice to me."

"You met their mothers? Already?"

She nods, "Mama boys the two of them."

Danielo gives a sexy grin. "I admit it."

Salvador shrugs, "Me too."

"We're daddy's girls, so we understand," I say, sipping my bubbly.

The men laugh.

"Your sister is funny, Corrie," Salvador, the spiky-haired one says. "I like her."

"Corrie?" I look at Corrine. "You have a nickname already?"

Salvador smiles shyly. "It's a work in progress."

"Should I be coming up with one for you?" Danielo leans over and his stubbly chin tickles my face. "I hear you're single."

I dagger Corrine with my eyes.

She shrugs. "Word got around as I was talking to Ava and Daisy on the phone."

"We met your sisters," Danielo says. "That young one, Emerald, is mean."

"What'd she tell you?" I love Emmie, I'm thinking.

"That she'd hunt me down if I hurt her sisters."

"Yeah, sounds like Emerald. She used to be a scaredy cat and now she's the complete opposite. So, what team do you guys play for?" I change the subject before they go back to my recent single status.

"Porto FC," they both shout, raising fists and making some kind of gang or tribal gesture.

"Oh, I see." Porto is where Corrine will be for a year. I'm not sure whether to be glad she'll know some people in Porto, or worried it's these football players.

"How long have you been playing soccer?" I ask Danielo.

Salvador is busy whispering and laughing with Corrine. They do look cute together. He towers over her even sitting down, and she gazes up at him with adoring eyes.

"Football, you mean."

"Right, football, sorry."

In the thirty more minutes it takes to reach our Airbnb, I've had two full glasses of bubbly, learned all about Danielo's position as a midfield striker, and told Danielo I will consider coming to see their game against Athens tomorrow night.

When the limo pulls up in front of the building, Danielo leaps out and reaches in to help me out.

He kisses my hand and declares, "It was my pleasure to meet you, Bridget. Until tomorrow night."

I giggle in response. It's a combination of the champagne, his romantic gesture, and his assumption that I am some kind of football groupie who can't wait to watch his muscular thighs run up and down an arena.

I turn around and wait for Corrine to say her goodbyes and join me on the sidewalk.

It's only then I notice a man standing in front of our apartment door. He's holding a large bouquet of roses. He's staring at me, and at my hand where Danielo kissed it, wearing a look I've never seen on his face before.

In mythology, Ajax is a large fierce warrior of great courage. But in the end, after all his heroic deeds, he was driven mad with disappointment.

That is the look I'm seeing now in my own Ajax's eyes. Tragic disappointment.

My heart stops beating knowing what he just witnessed. Which was not much really, but given where we left off, it looks like I have quickly moved on to another man.

I hurry over to tell him it was nothing, but he shakes off my hand.

"I knew I shouldn't have come," he says.

"Is this the famous Ajax?" Corrine walks up, bold and dauntless. "I'm Corrine. It's nice to meet the man who has broken our Bridget's heart."

He blanches.

I screech out, "Corrine!"

She shrugs. "Can we take this drama inside the apartment please?"

I numbly walk ahead and open the door with my key. When I turn around, it's only Corrine standing there with her carry-on.

"He had somewhere else to be," she says, her eyebrows drawn in. "I thought you said he was a nice guy."

"Thanks a lot," I groan at my sister. "You've ruined everything."

She pushes her way inside dragging her bag, "Thank God there's a/c, I'm dying! And darling, you ruined it all by yourself when you left Aegina."

Corrine is right. I ruined it. And now I must fix it.

Chapter Forty-Seven

AJAX

Our family home in Athens is two floors filled with art, books, and a grand piano.

It is where I'd planned to bring Bridget for a week of exploring this big city.

I don't have the energy to head back to the port and catch the last ferry home. Bridget with another man. I had not expected that.

She was laughing too. I wasn't going to spoil it for her. I liked seeing her smiling . . . even if it killed me to watch.

My phone buzzes and I ignore it. Exhaustion has caught up with me. The last week has taken its toll, for sure on my body, but mostly on my headspace. Nothing makes sense without Bridget. Absolutely nothing.

And now it looks like I'll have to find a way to make life make sense without her. But not right now. Right now, all I want is to go to sleep. For a long time.

So that's what I do. I put on my noise-canceling Airpods and I close my eyes.

I already know I'm going to dream about Bridget. Her smile and laugh have filled my dreams every night since she left Aegina.

My dreams are the only place I can be close to her. It's the only place I want to be right now.

Chapter Forty-Eight

BRIDGET

I can't sleep. I get out of bed before the sun comes up and make a cup of tea.

I sit staring at my phone, where hours ago I sent a long text to Ajax explaining what happened at the airport with Corrine and her new footballer friends giving us a ride.

I told him, I barely knew the man he saw kissing my hand. I apologized profusely, but my phone stayed as silent as a tomb. Ajax has not even read the messages I sent hours and hours ago.

"Face it," I moan to myself while sipping my hot tea. "I'm miserable without him. I have no idea how to make things right. I don't even know what right would look like. Maybe apologizing to him would be a start, but then what?"

"We'd be right back where we started. At odds because of long distance. Confused because we never really dated, we went from friends to fake fiancés and now we're . . . nothing. So weird," I mutter.

"What's so weird?" Corrine asks, trailing bed sheets behind her as she climbs onto the sofa next to me.

"I was thinking about Ajax."

"Cool. What're we going to do today?"

Corrine is not the dreamy sister who wants to analyze every little thing. That would be Daisy or Ava. Corrine and Emerald are the doers, the no-nonsense logical ones. Emerald may even have inherited Corrine's bad-boy obsession.

"I know you probably want to go sightseeing, and Athens has a lot to see, but I need to figure out what I'm going to do."

Corrine's face lights up as she scrolls through her phone.

"I got a message from Salvador. He wants to see me again."

"Can you focus on my situation?" I cry. "You have a whole year to find out if Salvador is as good as he looks."

She turns a shocked face my way. "I'm not planning to spend my year as a football groupie. As much as I love the whole sexy bad boy vibe, I want to change that about myself. I want to meet Portuguese artists, writers, and philosophers. I want to learn about the culture and the country's ideas."

Her eyes get a dreamy and faraway look. "That's why I'm traveling abroad. To expand my horizons."

"Poor man, I hope he knows. He looked like he wanted to wife you up ASAP."

Corrine laughs. "Um. No. I'm pretty sure they both play on and off the field."

I get up to put on the electric kettle to make more tea.

Corrine comes behind me, bed sheets trailing behind like she's some kind of runaway princess.

"And I did hear you. You need to figure out what to do. But about what?"

I pour out two cups of tea and wander back to the sofa. I hand Corrine one and she unwraps a package of crackers and hands me a few.

"About Ajax. I love him."

"Do you now? Well, Danielo has invited you and Salvador has

invited me to watch the big game at the stadium this evening. They've left tickets at the gate for us. And we're supposed to wear anything, but blue. Apparently, that's Athens team colors."

I stare at Corrine like she's grown two heads.

She nods enthusiastically. "Exciting right? A European football game and we know the players and have fantastic seats. Come on Bridget, I fly back to Porto tomorrow. This is the least you can do. Hang out with me. Let's have fun."

"I'm sorry. I appreciate you coming all this way to cheer me up. But how is this helping me figure out what to do?"

Corrine shrugs. "We can think about it while we watch the game. It's not as if you have any bright ideas right this minute."

She's right. I have zero bright ideas on how to fix my sad situation.

"Fine," I grumble. My sister has come all the way here to be supportive. Her idea of doing that is to distract me.

Later, as we ride the Hop On Hop Off colorful bus around Athens, jumping off whenever we get to some place we want to see more of, like the Monastiraki Square with its famous flea markets and restaurants, Corrine interrogates me about what I truly want from my relationship with Ajax.

"You can't figure out how to fix something if you don't know what you want to fix," she says as she flips through an array of colorful leather cat face purses.

"These are adorable. I'm buying one each for Daisy and Emerald."

I help her pick out the purple for Daisy and the yellow for Emerald. We continue walking between the narrow alleyways that loop through and around the neighborhood.

"If you ask me, Bridget, you're confused because you don't know who you are."

I stop in my tracks, "What did you say?"

Corrine pulls my arm and drags me along. She stops to look in a shop full of natural handmade olive oil soaps. The scent of the soap reminds me so much of Ajax and his family that tears spring to my eyes.

"I said, you don't know who you are or what you want. Like with your job. Did you truly want to be a content creator? Is that what you said to yourself when you were growing up? I want to be in marketing, promoting other people's products?"

"Nobody is doing what they dream of doing when they were kids."

Corrine frowns, "Excuse me, I am."

"You're still in college. You will change your mind once you get a real job."

Corrine frowns at me, "When did you give up, Bridge? When did you decide to stop doing the thing you love most in the world and settle for a 'job?'" She does air quotes.

"I like my job."

"But do you love it? I haven't been around you a lot recently. You were away at college, then I left for college, so it's been every Friday evening for dinner, and then it's family vacations during the summer, but you know what I've observed?"

"I'm afraid to ask."

She looks at me head-on. "You're sitting in the audience of your own life. You're avoiding the stage, literally and metaphorically. Why is that?" Corrine's arms are crossed, her shopping bags tucked under one arm, her eyes flashing at me. As if this was a beef she'd had with me for a long time and is only now raising it.

The truth is that these are the exact questions I've been asking myself.

"I . . . don't know . . . ," I stop, my words freezing on my lips.

"I think you do know. I think it has to do with being afraid. For the record, we're all afraid." Corrine is relentless. Maybe she should be a lawyer. Or a detective.

I scratch my head. "What do you think I'm afraid of?"

That Ajax will die, is what pops into my head. The fear I shared with Daisy. The fear I know well, but can't control.

She cocks her head, scary in her intensity. "I think you already know. It's okay to be afraid. It's not okay to hide behind your fears."

The Hop On Hop Off bus approaches the bus stop.

"It's time we head back and get ready for tonight," she says. "Unless there's someplace else that you'd like to see?"

We sit at the top of the bus and watch the magic of Athens go by. The land of great literature and myths, where democracy was founded, where classical drama was born.

"I want to show you the amphitheater," I blurt out.

THE ODEON IS MORE THAN A FAMOUS HISTORICAL landmark, I realize on my second visit to it. It's a beacon calling to me. The moment I reach the round black circular stage and step out into the center, I feel as if this is right where I need to be.

"This is where I belong," I say softly.

"I agree," Corrine whispers. She pulls out her phone and snaps photos of me. "You need to remember this is your true calling."

"For centuries, actors have crossed this stage, performing stories that entertain and teach lessons. The actor conveys the truths of the cosmos to the audience. This is what I want. Who I am."

Corrine looks relieved as I spin around on the stage. "Finally," she says. "I'm making a video so our sisters can see that you're where you need to be."

I grin. "This feels natural."

I recite a monologue from a Shakespeare play I learned in

college. People sit down and watch and listen, not realizing I'm only playing around with the ancient stage.

When I'm done, the growing audience claps their hands.

"Excuse me, miss, who are you? Can I get your autograph?"

Corrine raises her phone high to video me shaking hands.

One man says, "You're better than I've seen in theaters."

A smile inside me breaks loose. "Thank you, sir. Your words mean a lot."

I step down from the stage.

Corrine holds up her phone so I can see the screen. Our sisters are there. Ava, Daisy, and Emerald. Dad is in the background. "What's going on?" I ask.

"Oh, Bridget, I never thought I'd see you perform again. You're brilliant. What a waste to give up such talent." That's Ava being overly dramatic.

But then Dad seconds her saying, "Superb as always, Bridge. Your mother always said you belong on a stage. She'd be happy to see you on one of the oldest stages in the world."

"Whoa, guys, slow down."

"No, Bridget," Corrine declares. "You've been going slow for a while now. Stop playing small when you're a star."

A chorus of "Bridget is a star" resounds from Corrine's phone.

I burst into tears. "I'm sorry. I don't know how I got off track."

Dad makes soothing sounds. "It's okay, baby. Getting off track is part of your journey. It's never too late to get back on track. Your path is always there waiting for you. That's why it's called *your* path."

The screeching of traffic and zooming of motorbikes is loud over the sound of my sisters and father's voices.

The bright colors of Athens, the excessive city sounds, and the smell of fried foods, smoke, and diesel fill my head. Suddenly, I know the only place I want to be right this minute. It's not that far away.

I grab Corrine's arm. "Sis, I'm sorry to do this to you. But I've got someplace I need to be."

A smile breaks slowly across her face. I thought she'd be mad, but this is Corrine, the most independent Walker sister. She'll be fine in Athens at a football game on her own. Especially with Salvador at her beck and call.

"Go, Bridget," she hugs me close. "Go get your leading man."

Chapter Forty-Nine

AJAX

The early ferry is packed with day trippers to Aegina, but I've managed to get a ticket from a friend at one of the ticket booths.

"Standing room only," he warns me.

I shrug, "Doesn't matter."

I spend the first half hour at the railing staring out at the sea, feeling every wave that smacks the hull. Salt spray lashes my face, but I don't care. After two full days and nights holed up in the Athens apartment, nursing my broken heart, I need something harsh to wake me up from this sadness.

Now I'll have to go home and explain to everyone that I lost Bridget for good.

Her text message only apologized for showing up with another guy, it didn't say anything about us trying to work anything out. It's as if she's moved on and put Aegina and me behind her.

The sea turns as stormy as my heart and the captain tells everyone to come inside the boat.

I follow instructions, but I wish I could be standing outside holding the railing feeling every jolt and drop of rain bombarding the ferry.

I want to feel something. Anything. Even the thunderous rain would be better than this empty feeling of going home without my true love.

An hour later, I'm driving through the gates of Christos Olive Farm. The rain has stopped and the sun shines as if the storm never happened.

I stop the Jeep in the exact same spot where Bridget and I had stopped almost two months ago. I can't even recall how long it's been. It feels as if she was always here with me.

Finally, I get back in the Jeep and make my way to the house. As I park the vehicle and walk around to the patio facing the fields, I glimpse someone in bright blue standing on a ladder. Elena's voice is shouting something that sounds like English. Who would she be speaking English to?

I drop my car keys on the table.

"You're here!" Mama comes out of her office and approaches with a big smile.

"Why are you so happy?" I grumble. "The plan didn't work. Bridget is not coming back."

Mama shakes her head. "Trust in the Fates, my son. True love will always win."

I cock an eyebrow at her. "Um . . . if you're talking about me dating Iona now, I'm sorry Mama, I'm not ready to be with anyone at all. Not for a long time. And who's Elena talking to? Who's up on our ladder over there? Is that a new farm manager or something? Did you try to replace me after only a few days away?" I say the last part a little bitterly, but I don't mean it.

"Let's go meet your new employee," Mama says.

"You're joking, right? You and Papa didn't really hire someone else without my input." I stride toward the ladder and the sound of Elena's voice She sounds chipper and happy, but she's always loved being in the field with her graphs.

As Mama and I pass row after row of olive trees, I hear a voice I know well. My heart quickens. I race toward the voice, my heart beating faster and faster.

I've left Mama behind as I turn down the row of trees and see her. Straddling a ladder, balancing precariously while reaching out with clippers in her other hand.

I don't shout to distract her and cause a fall. Instead, I walk up slowly. Scared to death Bridget will fall off that ladder. Now I know how she felt when I was up there every day.

"Ajax?" Elena sees me and grins. "Look who's here!" She points at my beautiful angel in her blue overalls and a baseball cap on her head turned backward.

Bridget turns around, her hand holding the clipper slowly moving to her side.

"Don't move," I grab the ladder firmly. Making sure it's steady and not going to topple over. I look upwards and Bridget is haloed by the sun. I don't know what she's doing here, but my heart can barely contain itself inside my body.

"Can you climb down please or do I need to come up there?"

She smiles. "I like the view up here."

"Fine." I climb up the rungs slowly making sure we're safe. When I get near the top and can see into her eyes, my heart revs up even more.

"What are you doing here?" I whisper, afraid this is a dream.

With her head tilted to one side, the sun slanting off her gorgeous face, her throat dark and creamy, waiting for my kisses, she says, "I love you. Do you still love me?"

I nod afraid to speak.

"Somebody had to handle your chores while you were taking a break in Athens."

"Taking a break, huh? Is that what we're calling this . . . thing that happened?" I choke out.

She smiles the sunniest smile. "We have a long time to figure out what to call it."

Skepticism clouds my face. "Meaning?"

"Meaning you need help, dude. I'm here to help. We have a lot of work to do before the agritours will be ready to go. With your family's guidance."

My head is spinning and I'm afraid we'll fall off the ladder. "Can we get down please?"

"Are you kidding? We're only getting started. It's straight to the top, darling."

Elena laughs. "Yeah, Ajax, straight to the top."

I'm so frightened to say the next words but I have to say them. "What about us?"

She reaches out and plucks a small olive branch from the tree. Extending it to me, she says solemnly, "Ajax Christos, will you please accept my peace offering? I am sorry for what I put you through. You are the man I'm meant to be with. And I know you may need some time to forgive me for running out and being dense and stubborn and refusing to commit and all the fearful things old Bridget was about, but I am here now.

"And I'm hoping, maybe in addition to me working with your family on the farm tours, you might want to start dating me. Officially."

The questions swimming in her dark brown eyes hurtle straight at my heart. Her words spin circles in my head.

"Is this true?" I ask, looking down at Mama and Papa who has rolled up on his trusty tractor. "Bridget is staying to help with the farm?"

Papa nods. Mama smiles. Elena claps her hands.

I turn back to Bridget, "What about your family in Portland?"

"They're 100 percent behind this plan. If I come home after the harvest to visit. So, I was thinking . . . if you'd like to be my official boyfriend, we can tell them by video call later."

I reach for her hand. "Give me the clippers."

"What?"

"Give me the clippers. Let's get down from this ladder."

When we're on the ground, she turns around, her eyes wide. "Well?"

I shake my head. "No, Bridget, I'm sorry. I can't do that. I don't want to be your boyfriend."

Chapter Fifty

BRIDGET

If the earth could open right now and pull me under, I'd go gladly. Pity wells in Elena's eyes. Mr. Christos shakes his head and Mrs. Christos covers her face in her hands.

"We're so sorry, Bridget," they say, but their voices are muffled by the loud droning noise in my ears.

Tears heat the backs of my eyelids.

I turn away and run. Zigzagging through the olive trees, past the fence, and out into the meadow I discovered on my first day on Aegina when everything was different. When there was promise and hope and excitement of seeing Ajax again.

I sink down in the sun-warmed grass and cry. Did I really think it'd be easy for him to forgive me?

I foolishly thought I could show up and make everything okay with my declaration of love. My big plans. How presumptuous.

"Bridget?"

My head whips around to see Ajax approaching. He probably wants to make sure I'm on the next ferry off his island.

"What?" I hiccup. I know my face is smeared with dirt from

working in the fields. Not to mention, my hair is frizzy from the humidity and heat.

"What are you doing here?" he asks.

The sides of my mouth droop downwards. "Saying goodbye."

"Goodbye?"

I look him in the eye. Is he playing a game with me?

"I heard you loud and clear, Ajax. No need for us to have a do-over. I'm ashamed and embarrassed I ran off on you. I understand why you don't want to be my boyfriend."

He slides down in the grassy field, sitting close to me, stretching his muscled legs out in front of him.

His closeness is torture. I want to bury my face in his shoulder, beg for his forgiveness, and ask if we can start over. But I respect his answer. No, can do.

"Bridget, are you listening to me or are you daydreaming?"

I jolt up, shoulders squared. "I'm listening, I guess."

"Okay." He gently turns my chin towards his face. I lose myself in his deep dark eyes.

"Yes?" I whisper. "What're you doing?"

A smile slides across his lips. "I don't want to be your boyfriend, Bridget."

My head drops. It feels too heavy for my poor neck. How many times do I need to hear his rejection?

"I know," I whisper.

"I don't want to be your boyfriend, because I want to be your husband."

My head springs up fast like a jack-in-the-box toy. "What?"

He pulls out a stunning dark blue ring with tiny diamonds embedded in the band. He picks up my left hand while I stare. "Bridget Walker, will you do me the honor of being my wife one day? I'll wait until you're ready. However long it takes. I cannot live my life without you. You are the woman I adore. The only woman I love *now and forever*."

"Your wife?" I sound like a parrot.

He nods. "Yes, the engagement can be as long as you — as we — want. But I want to commit to you here and now. No more games, no more fake anything. You're the woman for me and I want you by my side in everything we do. From agritours to trips back to Portland to traveling the world. Will you please say yes?"

I stare at the ring in his fingers.

I take a beat. So much has happened in the past days. So many things have reversed themselves in my mind, that my heart is still playing catch up.

But the thing my heart knows without a doubt is that it can't bear to be without Ajax nearby.

"Yes. My answer is yes, I want to commit to you all the way. I want to be your fiancée and your wife. I want to be yours forever."

A waterfall of a smile gushes from him as he shouts, "Hallelujah!" and gathers me in his arms.

"You've made me the happiest man in the world today! And every day to come."

I squeeze my eyelids closed. Press my face against his strong chest.

"Mom, do you see me? I did it. I've given my heart to Ajax. With your blessing," I whisper to the sky above Ajax's head.

An unusually strong breeze blows through the meadow. Maybe it's Mom saying she's proud of me.

Ajax wraps both arms around me tightly.

I feel so protected, loved, and adored. How did I ever turn my back on this joy?

"Let's go share our news," he says excitedly, pulling me up.

Ten minutes later, we find Elena under one of the olive trees.

"You guys?" Elena runs to us wide-eyed and hopeful.

Ajax pulls her ponytail. "Thank you for all your help getting two old fuddy-duddies to see the light."

I bend down and hug Elena. "Thank you, sweetie. We're going to be sisters for real."

At the squeals of joy coming from their youngest child, Mr. and Mrs. Christos hurry outside. I wave my ring finger in the air.

My new family cheers for us. Then, we head inside to call the rest of the family — my sisters and Dad and Maxine in Portland, and Corrine in Portugal. Without them, I would never have found the happiness that I finally believe I deserve.

Chapter Fifty-One

BRIDGET

"Babe, are you almost ready?" Ajax's voice sounds high-pitched with nerves.

"I'm coming honey, hold on." I swab my lips with more lip gloss, and fluff out my curls, which have grown so long on Aegina.

I flew back home at the end of my three months to apply for a visa to stay longer in Greece. Thankfully, the Greek Embassy stamped its approval, and I returned in time for the harvest. Somehow, with all that was going on, I never made it to a salon for a haircut.

After our small engagement celebration with only a few family members — no more big productions for us — Ajax and I settled into a daily routine that was anything but boring.

The first thing we did was go around individually to the family scattered across Aegina and tell them about the agritours we planned for Christos Farms.

Unlike my idea of promoting the products through social

media only, which was an epic fail, everyone loves the tours. It was Iona's idea, but I've organized the details and the advertising.

As Uncle Theo put it, "You can show them how to make the oil and I can sell them the oil afterward."

"Exactly," I smiled at him. "We'll create a tour that takes real-life visitors through the process of olive oil production, from tree to table. And at the end of the tour, there will be an olive oil tasting."

"With our delicious bread," says one of the aunts.

"Exactly! Your daily homemade bread will be used at the end of the tour for product testing."

"Ju ju can show them all his new ideas for protecting water and the soil as a farmer."

I thought I could keep my regular job remotely, but ended up having to resign and concentrate on Christos Farms. Creating a tour, getting permits and licenses, and organizing all the promotions is a full-time job.

Elena suggested we offer private picnic basket lunches in the meadow near the trees for those who want to do something else after the tour or instead of the tour.

The Aegina winemakers have asked me to help create a wine tour for their vineyards. It looks like I will have a lot of work to do for a long while.

Of course, the most important part of the farm was the olive harvest in October.

I couldn't believe how much fun it was. Everyone in the family, from the youngest of five years to the oldest at seventy-five, arrived with jeans, boots, and gloves on their hands.

Nets were spread around the trees and then the shaking began.

"What is happening?" I asked, watching in delight as the strongest of the men, which included Ajax, shook the trees so hard that olives came tumbling down on my head.

The women and children scooted onto the nets, removing the leaves and twigs.

I was amongst them, hurrying to separate the olives from the leaves.

"Now what?" I asked winded as the tractor came by and collected the large tubs of olives we'd poured from the nets.

"We move to the next row," Ajax laughed. "Are you tired yet?"

"Wait," I said, short of breath. "We have to do this to all the trees in every single row?"

He nodded, leaning over to kiss my dry lips. "You got this Pong. I know how competitive you are."

I shake my head. "I'm advertising this as the highlight of the tours during October. Visitors can help us shake down the trees and gather the olives. They'll love it."

"The more the merrier, sweetheart. As long as you're near to me, I'm happy."

"I'm never leaving you again, mister."

I tilt my head to press my mouth on his yummy lips. How could I ever imagine a world where Ajax and I don't get to kiss at least ten times each day?

The harvest season is over. The olives were pressed the same day they were picked. The oil was declared to be of superb quality.

Mr. Christos hugged me and said, "You belong on this island, Bridget." Which as far as I was concerned was the highest praise I could ever receive from him.

Now that it's over, Ajax said he had a surprise for me. I have no idea what it could be, but I'm happy to dress up and put on some makeup.

I admit I've had enough of shaking trees and ducking from olives pelting down on my head. The bottle and my newly designed labels look awesome, and I can't wait to taste the oil I helped to pick.

"You ready, Bridget? We're going to miss it."

I hurry out of my bedroom and find Ajax standing there looking like a Greek model. Fine white linen shirt, a dark blue suit, and a smile that makes my heart leap.

"Wow! I can't believe you're my man."

His eyes sweep over my clingy red dress and his jaw drops down. "You mean, I can't believe I get you to myself."

"Only for tonight," I tease. "We have a lot to do tomorrow. The tours will be starting with our brand-new batch of olive oil."

He snorts, "Woman stop thinking about work. It's time for some fun."

"Where're we going? Give me a hint."

He hitches up one eye and screws his lips crookedly. "If I tell you, will you stop bugging me?"

I smile widely, "I knew I'd get you to break."

"Don't tell her Ajax," Elena says as she runs over to check out my dress and heels. I swirl around to give her the full effect. She'd helped me pick out the dress in town two days ago.

"You look like a movie star."

After kisses and waves, we head out. Sitting next to Ajax in his freshly cleaned Jeep, I can't help but admire his profile. His chiseled chin, the dimples that pop out unexpectedly when he showers me with a wide smile. But mostly, his cool vibe that melds so perfectly with my frantic one and calms me down.

With him, I've learned to trust myself, to listen to nature, to watch the stars and float on the water. Ajax is everything and more I could ever hope for in a future husband.

"What are you thinking about so hard?" he asks as we drive through the fast-approaching sunset.

"I'm thanking the Greek gods for their crazy dramatic way of getting us together."

He smiles and dimples appear.

"That's wonderful. Because we're going to see a few of those gods right now."

The next thing I know, we're on a ferry heading to Athens. The sun is setting as we head across the Gulf towards the big city.

Ajax is carrying a backpack on his back that does not go with his suit.

"Well?" I ask looking into his eyes. "When are you going to tell me?"

He smiles mysteriously and pulls me into the shelter of his arms. "Patience, my darling."

I sigh. "This better be good."

And it is!

The giant arches of the ancient Odeon Theater are backlit in purple and gold. The sun is setting all the way down as multicolored lights shine from the pathways to the ancient stone seats.

"What's going on?" I breathe. My heart is racing with excitement. "Is there a show?"

He grins. "Welcome to Greek theater, my love."

I press a hand to my heart where it seems like it's trying to burst through my skin. Tears well up in my eyes. "We're going to see a show?"

He nods his head as he leads me carefully down the stone steps to a perfect spot on the left of the stage where we can see everything on the black dais as clearly as can be.

He zips open the backpack and pulls out two seat cushions and a blanket.

Ajax clears his throat. "I know you miss the big city life with the fancy stuff. But I want you to know I will make sure we come here at least once a month. To visit Athens and the other cities. For theater and concerts. Whatever you want to see or do. Because, Bridget Walker, you deserve to have the best of both worlds. I'm incredibly happy you chose to be in mine."

I'm full-on crying now, dabbing at my eyes with the bandana Ajax produces from his suit pocket. The bandana and suit combo aside, I love my man so much.

I swallow my tears so I can thank him properly, "I already have the best of everything with you, my love," I tell him honestly.

He presses his lips together. "I'm so lucky."

I nod. "Me, too."

Oedipus Rex is a play I know well. But I've never seen it performed. I'm so mesmerized by the actors, the chorus, and the theatrics I can't quell the surge of excitement thrumming through my body.

"Ajax," I whisper. "Now that the harvest is over and the tours are all planned, is there some free time?"

His arm is wrapped around my shoulders. The stars gleam in the night sky.

"You mean after we return from our Portland visit?"

"Yes."

"Sure."

"Because I'm going to start an English theater in Aegina."

He leans back. I feel his eyes on me in the dark. I can't see his features but under the glow of purple lights I see the white smile lighting up his face.

"I think I can convince the committee that runs the Municipal Theater to allow me to stage some plays and musicals in English."

"Since Iona is on that committee, I think you can. She has a lot of respect for you for committing to an island life and to a farm even though you're a city girl."

I chuckle. "Only because this is where you are, Ajax Christos."

He kisses the tip of my nose.

I watch the rest of the Greek tragedy in utter fascination. I'm here, with the man I love, watching authentic Greek theater. I'm going to start my own production company. And I'll perform in the plays myself.

My life is overflowing with gifts from the Greek gods.

It's so true, as the author informed me in her book. *You can't have a sunrise without a sunset.*

I've put my past fears to rest. I'm preparing for a lot of sunrises.

Ajax rests his head on top of mine.

"Let me know how I can help, baby."

I nod watching the actors suffer on stage because their hubris insults the gods.

I'll have to be careful. I must remember to always be grateful. I'm living in the land of Greek gods after all.

DEAR READER,

I hope you enjoyed the story. Please Leave a Review on Amazon to help others find this book! It would mean a lot to me (and to Bridget & Ajax!). It can be as short as you want! I look forward to reading your thoughts!

Thank you,

Lynn

Lynn Joseph is from Trinidad & Tobago. When she's not writing her international romances, she can be found on a beach somewhere in the world. Or binge-watching *Hart of Dixie* and *The Vampire Diaries* over and over. Lynn lives in charming South Portland, Maine, and on the Caribbean Island of Tobago, where she's known as the Mermaid Queen. Join her on her journey of love, food, and romantic destinations (not necessarily in that order). www.lynnjosephbooks.com

Stay Connected

Sign up for Lynn's newsletter and receive a FREE ebook, *Princess Aboard.* Plus be in the know for all the behind the scenes goodies and more!

Sign Up Here —>
https://BookHip.com/NKSQGRS

Follow her on social media:

Facebook -http://facebook.com/lynnjosephauthor
Instagram - https://www.instagram.com/lynnjosephbooks/
Bookbub - https://bit.ly/3Phcsuu
Amazon - https://amzn.to/3VTd8Kb
Goodreads -https://bit.ly/4gUtZo4

Lynn loves to hear from her readers and invites them to email her, anytime at lynn@lynnjosephbooks.com

www.lynnjosephbooks.com

Also by Lynn Joseph

The Walker Sisters Forever Series

(Sweet Romance)

Gelato Forever

Olives Forever

Sangria Forever

Paris Forever

Christmas Forever

Cocoa Reef Resort Series

(Steamy Romance)

Lime to My Coconut

Rum to the Reggae

Spice for My Santa

Princess Abroad

(Read for FREE! —> https://BookHip.com/NKSQGRS)